Y0-BED-849

"Remember what I asked you before?" Chelsea pressed. "You said I should think it over for a while."

"Oh, that," Connor said, his voice suddenly serious.

Chelsea laced her fingers through his. "I . . . I can't stand worrying that you might get deported," she whispered.

"I don't love the idea myself," he said sarcastically.

"I'm serious, Connor. I don't want to lose you."

"I'm pretty quick on my feet," he reassured her.

Chelsea hesitated. "But we'll never be able to relax," she said at last. "It could happen any day, at any time."

"That's my life," Connor said quietly. "That's the truth of it."

"It doesn't have to be," Chelsea argued. "You know there's one way to make you legal."

"Chelsea—"

She kissed him again, quieting him, though her own heart was pounding. "I'm asking you, Connor. Will you marry me?"

Don't miss any of the titles in the **making waves**
series by Katherine Applegate

making waves

sweet

katherine applegate

17th Street Press
New York

For Michael, who makes it fun.

The sale of this book without its cover is unauthorized. If you purchased this book without a cover, you should be aware that was reported to the publisher as "unsold and destroyed." Neither the author nor the publisher has received payment for the sale of this "stripped book."

 Published by
17th Street Press
an imprint of
17th Street Productions
an Alloy Online, Inc. company
151 West 26th Street
11th Floor
New York, NY 10011

Copyright © 1993, 2001 by 17th Street Productions and Katherine Applegate
Cover copyright © 2001 17th Street Productions
Cover photography by Garry Wade/Stone.
Cover design by Lauren Monchik.

All rights reserved. No part of this book may be reproduced or transmitted in any form or by any means, electronic or mechanical, including photocopying, recording, or by any information storage and retrieval system, without the written permission of the Publisher, except where permitted by law.

The trademark 17th Street Press is a trademark of 17th Street Productions, an Alloy Online, Inc. company. All rights reserved.

ISBN: 1-931497-14-1

Manufactured in the United States of America

First 17th Street Press Books printing June 2001

Originally published by HarperCollins Publishers as
Ocean City: Fireworks

10   9   8   7   6   5   4   3   2   1

one

"Ladies, I'm afraid I'm going to have to ask you to put your tops back on."

Justin Garrett stood with his arms crossed over his bare chest, feet planted firmly in the blistering sand. One of the two teenage girls splayed on the nearby beach blanket looked up at him, shading her eyes against the brilliant noon sun. She smiled and said something Justin couldn't understand, waving her hand expressively. The sweet smell of coconut suntan oil wafted toward him.

"There's no nude sunbathing on this beach," Justin said.

The second girl sat up. *"Qu'est-ce qu'il dit?"*

"Je ne comprend pas," said the first girl, shrugging.

French, or at least French Canadian, Justin guessed. Ocean City got a lot of Canadian tourists. Great. This was not a situation that could be handled intelligently with sign language. Justin gazed toward the water, carefully scanning his two hundred meters of shoreline.

When he looked back down at the girls, a shadow had fallen across them.

"Need a hand?" Alec Daniels asked, deadpan. Alec was a fellow lifeguard and a housemate of Justin's for the summer.

"I think I can deal with it."

Alec shook his head, fighting a grin. "I thought I'd better get a closer look at the problem."

"Yeah, I'll bet you did," Justin said. "This is *my* section of the beach, Daniels."

Alec pursed his lips. "I wasn't so sure. It looks to me like it's right on the line. And I didn't want to shirk my duties."

Justin looked back down at the girls, trying very hard to keep his eyes focused on their faces. Fortunately he was wearing dark sunglasses. "Does either of you speak English?"

"Non, je suis desolée," the first girl said, cocking her head. *"Nous sommes françaises."* Then, in a heavy accent, she added, "French."

"Great," Justin muttered. "You need to wear a top," he said, making a pantomime of picking something up with both hands and tying it in back of his neck.

Alec snickered. The girls exchanged mystified looks.

"Ils sont beaux, tous les deux, hein?" the second girl observed.

"She said we're handsome," Alec said. "Both of us. Although I'm pretty sure they were just being nice to you."

"You speak French?" Justin asked.

"A little," Alec admitted. "Two years in high school."

"Then tell them to put their tops back on," Justin said, exasperated.

"Do I have to?"

"It is the law. If we don't tell them, the cops will."

"What a shame." Alec sighed, then attempted an explanation in stumbling French.

After a moment the girls began retying their bikini tops, their rapid-fire conversation heavily punctuated by giggles and rolled eyes.

"What are they saying?" Justin asked.

"I'm not getting it all, but the general idea seems to be that we're immature and ridiculous, and that a man with any sophistication would be able to handle the sight of a woman's breasts."

"Wonderful," Justin said flatly. "I always like to make a good impression." He turned back toward his lifeguard chair, waving over his shoulder to Alec. "Later."

It had been a slow day so far. The surf was breaking softly, and even the gulls, wheeling and dodging overhead, seemed less offensive than usual. There was a good crowd on the beach, but they'd been a well-behaved bunch by and large.

Justin kept his gaze on the water as he walked, taking note of everyone in his section. The old, fish-belly-white man staring out to sea and smoking a cigar as the waves lapped at his waist. The young boy trying out a snorkel and mask in too shallow water. The high school couple a hundred yards out, arms linked across an air mattress, kissing and laughing.

At the water's edge two little girls were taking Barbie and Ken on a date to a sand castle. A blond boy, seven or eight, hovered near the castle, no doubt plotting his demolition strategy.

Justin climbed back onto his white wooden perch. "Immature and ridiculous, huh?" he muttered. He grinned and once again began his methodical scanning of the water.

He heard a chorus of shouts and looked over to see the little blond boy launch a sneak attack on Barbie's sand castle. The boy raced off down the beach, the two little girls and their dolls in hot pursuit. He hadn't gone far when he slammed into the legs of a middle-aged man wearing a Dodgers baseball cap. The man laughed good-naturedly, and the boy sped on.

Justin returned his gaze to the sea. Something

nagged at him, though. He glanced back at the man in the cap. He was wearing dark sunglasses; he was thin, not very tan, and long legged. And he seemed to be looking at Justin. Staring. Justin furrowed his brow, staring back. But the man's face was lost in the bright glare of the sun.

"Where's the nearest bathroom?"

The voice, coming from just below his chair, startled Justin. He looked down at a mother holding a squirming toddler in her arms.

Justin gave her directions, and by the time he looked back, the middle-aged man had vanished.

"Disgusting," Chelsea Lennox muttered, peering into the greasy white paper bag she'd carried down the length of the boardwalk. She wrinkled her nose at the briny smell. Vile things, soft-shell crabs. You could slap all the mayo in the world on one and it would still look like a big fried spider. Still, Connor loved them, and she loved Connor, and people did funny things in the name of love.

She paused in front of a rough plywood fence that surrounded a construction site and rocked back on her heels. The bare steel bones of a new hotel towered above her. Several people were working on the fourth floor, but with the searing noon sun directly overhead, she couldn't tell if Connor was among them.

Chelsea made her way along the fence, which was plastered with bright posters and announcements. A new bingo parlor was opening next to the Little Indy Go-Kart Track. Bus trips to the Atlantic City casinos were leaving daily. A psychic over on the bay side was offering a two-for-one special on tarot-card readings.

Chelsea made a note to keep that last poster in mind. She wouldn't mind a glimpse into her future. Maybe she could talk Kate into the two-for-one deal, but it seemed unlikely. Best friend or not, Kate wasn't the tarot-card type.

From beyond the fence came the sounds of construction equipment, diesel engines overwhelming the noise of the noontime crowd. The beach was packed. On the way over she'd passed Alec and Justin, two of her housemates, at their lifeguard stations. Poor guys had their work cut out for them today.

A guard was at the gate, an old man wearing a dusty gray uniform and cap. "Where you going?" he asked brusquely.

"I want to see a friend. I brought him lunch." Chelsea held up her greasy bag as proof.

"Who's the friend?"

"Connor Riordan. He's an Irish guy."

"An Irishman, you say?" The man laughed

dryly. "That doesn't exactly narrow it down, not on this site." He looked at her sideways, a faint shadow of disapproval in his eyes. Chelsea was getting used to that look. Some people still couldn't handle the idea of a black girl and a white guy together.

"I guess it's okay," the old man decided at last. "They're about to blow the lunch whistle, anyway." He jerked his head twice. "Go on in, only be careful."

He handed her a battered yellow hard hat. Chelsea gazed at it reluctantly. She was wearing a blue sarong with a matching cover-up over a matching tank suit. "Do I have to?" she asked. "I'm trying to make a fashion statement here." When the man didn't answer, she sighed and put on the hard hat.

Making her way over torn earth and scattered bits of steel and wire, Chelsea spotted Connor. He and two other workmen were climbing into a rickety-looking wire cage on the third floor.

"Connor!" she yelled. "Down here."

He looked down, found her, and laughed as the cage began moving upward. Connor shrugged helplessly. "I'll send the lift back down to you. Come on up," he yelled. "I'll be on the fourth floor. Just push the red button."

Chelsea waited for the elevator to climb to

the top, then descend again slowly. She stepped in and punched the button. With a sudden jerk it rattled and took off, rising swiftly and bringing the teeming beach and placid ocean beyond it into view. A gull hung in the air, eyeing her, no doubt aware, as any beach-wise gull would be, that white paper bags almost always held food.

The elevator stopped with another jerk, and Chelsea climbed out shakily. Connor took her in his arms and hugged her close. His bare skin was hot and dry from the sun. He'd had this job only a little while, but already she could see changes in him. His shoulders were red and freckled, his arms hardened with new muscles. His bleached-out curls glinted with gold streaks where they escaped his hard hat.

Connor leaned down and gave her a lingering kiss. One of his coworkers whistled, and it echoed loudly against the bare concrete.

"What are you doing here?" Connor asked. "Tired of playing beach photographer? Looking for a real job?"

"I brought lunch. Soft-shell sandwiches for you, a veggie pita for me. Thought I'd surprise you."

"You not only surprised me, you saved my life," he said enthusiastically. "The lunch I packed today managed to get stepped on by a clumsy fellow with big boots. Me."

He led her across the bare concrete floor. Someday this would be a hotel, with walls and carpets and maids carrying fresh towels. Now it looked like a parking garage, slabs of concrete with nothing to keep out the fresh ocean breeze. The two workmen who had ridden up in the elevator with Connor were sitting at the edge. Their legs dangled over the side as they unwrapped their sandwiches and admired the girls on the beach below.

Connor and Chelsea sat on overturned plastic drums, and she began handing out the food. Connor finished off a sandwich in a matter of seconds.

"So," Chelsea said, grinning as he gulped down a slug of lemonade, "I guess you've been working hard today."

"Good honest labor," Connor said. "Too bloody much good honest labor. We're shorthanded, although I can't complain, can I? If the boss weren't shorthanded, he wouldn't be hiring the likes of me."

Chelsea tilted her head and admired the way his stomach stayed flat and hard as he hunched over to grab a handful of french fries. "I kind of think the hard work agrees with you."

Connor smiled, his eyes traveling over her body. "You don't look bad yourself."

Chelsea shrugged. "Oh, this old thing?" She

tugged at the strap of her tank suit. "This is just my uniform."

"Nice uniform. How's business?"

"Pretty good. It's wall-to-wall tourists today, and everybody wants a video of the family splashing around in the surf. My boss says I'm—"

"Ah, hell!"

Chelsea turned to see the two other construction workers jump to their feet, muttering curses. One of them waved urgently at Connor. "Immies! They're checking green cards."

Connor leaped up, crumpling the paper bag of food into a ball and tossing it toward a pile of debris. "The tool locker, quick!" he said. He motioned the two workmen toward a steel tool locker the size of a small closet. "I'll lock the two of you in. They won't have a key, and besides, they won't think it's possible you could lock yourselves in from the outside."

While Chelsea watched anxiously, Connor led the two men over to the vertical box full of picks and shovels and rivet guns. They squeezed inside. "What about you, Con?" one of the men asked.

Connor shut the door and closed the heavy lock. "I've got an idea. Don't worry."

"Connor, what's going on?" Chelsea demanded, grabbing his arm.

"Just a little visit from Immigration," Connor

replied lightly. He reached for her hand and pulled her along with him. "They're checking for illegal aliens. It happens a couple of times a summer."

They headed for a corner of the half-built building. When they reached the edge, Chelsea reeled back, struck by a wave of dizziness.

The elevator machinery growled into gear, carrying the Immigration men. "We have to hurry," Connor urged. "You're not afraid of heights, are you?"

"Actually—"

"Well, wait here and just don't look down."

Connor gazed overhead for a moment, then leaped straight up. Chelsea gasped as he caught the lip of a horizontal steel I beam and swung back and forth. On the backswing he grunted, heaved his legs up over his head, and disappeared.

Chelsea heard a scrabbling sound, and a second later a rope with a loop tied in the end appeared, dangling before her.

"Quick," Connor whispered. "Stand in the loop and hold on."

Chelsea gazed at the rope, horrified.

Nearby the elevator cables whirred. The Immigration people were getting closer. In a few seconds they would reach this floor. Then it would be too late. They'd see her. They'd know she wasn't alone. They'd find Connor and deport him back to Ireland.

Chelsea stuck her foot in the loop, wrapped both hands around the rough, prickly rope, and said a quick prayer. Instantly she began to ease clear of the floor, swinging several feet out over the abyss.

The rope rose in labored jerks until Chelsea was able to see Connor's boots. She clutched the ledge. Connor grabbed her under the arms and hauled her up in one smooth motion. Below her she heard the elevator rattle to a stop.

Connor took her in his arms. They were standing on a three-foot-wide ledge that extended to the end of the building. Chelsea peeked over her shoulder and nearly fainted. They were forty feet up, with a panoramic view of the beach that some hotel patron would soon enjoy—from behind the safety of a window.

"Don't look," Connor said softly. "Keep your eyes closed and don't think about it."

"What *else* am I supposed to think about?" she demanded in a hoarse whisper.

"Think about this," Connor murmured. He held her close and kissed her deeply, so deeply, she almost forgot everything else.

two

Chelsea snapped off the bedside lamp and lay still, letting her eyes adjust to the shadows. Pale moonlight spilled through her curtains, whispering with the warm bay breeze. Yellow light from the hall sliced under the crack beneath her door, etching a path across her floor. There was an interesting picture there somewhere, Chelsea thought, eyeing the spot where the sharp knife of light melted into the soft pool of moonlight. She started to reach for her sketch pad, then stopped herself. It had been a tough day, and she was exhausted. The drawing could wait until morning.

But as soon as she closed her eyes, the picture vanished. Suddenly all Chelsea could see was the ledge, high above the beach, where she'd clung to Connor in terror that afternoon.

A few seconds and he would have been gone from her life. It happened quickly, he'd said, laughing as if it were no big deal—they carded you, then arrested you, and within days you were aboard an airplane on your way back to Ireland, never able to come to America again.

Someone knocked lightly on her door, and Chelsea opened her eyes. "Yes?"

"It's me. Kate."

"Come on in." Chelsea raised herself onto one elbow.

Kate opened the door. Her blond hair caught the light and glowed like a halo around her head. "Do you have my gray V-necked shirt?" she asked.

Chelsea thought for a moment. "It's in the laundry. Sorry, I haven't gotten around to doing a load lately."

"No big deal," Kate said, shrugging. "I'll find something else to wear tomorrow." She turned to leave.

"Hey, Kate?"

Kate looked back. "Yeah?"

Chelsea hesitated. "Never mind. Nothing."

But Kate didn't leave. "What?" she asked, moving closer, her arms crossed over her chest.

"I wanted to ask you something," Chelsea said. She fingered the edge of her sheet. "But now it seems kind of dumb."

Kate sat on the edge of the bed, her eyes narrowing. "All right, spill it, Chels. You've been in space all evening."

Chelsea sat up, piling a pillow behind her back. "I was just wondering what it's like between you and Justin. You know, the whole thing."

"You mean sex?" Kate's eyebrows shot up.

Chelsea laughed. "That, too, but mostly I meant what it's like being so completely, well, *together.*"

"That's kind of tough to answer," Kate said with a sigh. "There's still so much stuff hanging over our relationship. Like what we're going to do at the end of summer, when he sails off in one direction and I head to college in the other."

"Okay, but for *now* what's it like?" Chelsea pressed. "I mean, I know you've been spending most nights down at the boathouse with Justin, which means you're practically living with him—"

"We are not," Kate said uncertainly. "I mean, living together . . ."

"Do you think about seeing other guys?"

"No," Kate admitted.

"And you have sex, like, constantly, right?"

Kate laughed. "Do you have a point, or are you just indulging your strange fascination with other people's sex lives?"

"Do you like it?"

"Like what? Sex? Or being in love with Justin?"

"Both."

"Yes and yes. All right?"

Chelsea watched the curtains ride the breeze. "Doesn't being so close to Justin sometimes make you feel like you're giving up your independence?"

"In some ways, I guess. One day I was just thinking about what *I* wanted, and the next day it had become . . . *we*. But I'm not too worried about that."

"But how can you stand not knowing how long it will last?" Chelsea asked urgently. "I mean, it could end, right?"

"Are you trying to depress me?" Kate asked. "Because you're doing a good job." She paused. "I guess I try not to think about the summer ending," she continued. "I figure I'll have to deal with that when it comes."

"But what if it wasn't a particular time like the end of summer?" Chelsea asked. "What if you had to worry that at any moment it could suddenly be over, like that?" She snapped her fingers.

"You know, Chelsea, I came in here feeling pretty good," Kate said with a teasing frown.

"Sorry." Chelsea smiled. "Since you're Miss Experienced with all this true love stuff, I thought you might have some wisdom to share."

"Are you worried that you and Connor won't last?"

Chelsea shrugged. "Sometimes. Other times I worry we will." It wasn't quite the truth, but then, Connor had made it clear he didn't want the fact that he was an illegal alien broadcast throughout the house. "So," Chelsea said mischievously, "on that other topic. Is it always great?"

After Kate left, Chelsea lay in bed, watching the shadows weave together and unravel. She had a good eye; her art teacher in high school had said so. Well, "quirky vision" was what he'd actually said, but Chelsea had taken it as a compliment. She noticed patterns and shapes and colors. Her artwork, no matter how "quirky," made a certain sense.

But when she looked at her own life, the patterns blurred; the colors muddied. Nothing made sense. She didn't have a vision of her future. Not even a quirky one.

On the other side of the wall she could hear the sound of the springs on Connor's bed as he climbed in. He was in the next room, only a few feet away. Chelsea threw back the covers and stood. The hardwood floor was cool beneath her bare feet. She groped in the dark for her bathrobe and slipped it on.

Maybe Kate could stand not knowing what would happen with Justin. But at least she had the luxury of looking ahead toward a particular month and day, with lots of time in between. If Justin went, it would be with tearful farewells. Connor would simply disappear.

Chelsea padded along the ratty hallway runner, stopping in front of Connor's door. His light was off. Except for the beating of her heart, the house was still. She put a shaky hand on the doorknob and slowly twisted it open.

Inside his room the air smelled of leather and books and the lime-scented aftershave he sometimes used. She took a deep breath, slipped inside, and closed the door behind her.

"Connor?" she whispered.

The only answer was his steady breathing.

She inched forward, feeling her way through the blackness. "Connor?" she whispered again, more insistently.

Her toe touched a trailing end of bedspread, and she stopped. The sound of his breathing was very near now. She reached down with her fingers and felt the edge of his bed. As her eyes adjusted to the dark, she could make out the shape of his body, uncovered from the waist up. He was lying on his back, head turned toward her.

She touched his cheek. His eyes flew open, but he lay perfectly still, waiting.

"It's me, Chelsea," she whispered.

A hand took hers and drew her closer. She sat on the bed, overwhelmingly conscious of his body so near.

Without a word he pulled her to him, kissing her deeply. It was so intense that for a moment she didn't notice the other hand that pulled the front of her bathrobe open.

She pulled back. "That's *not* what I came in here for," she told him, shaking her head.

"It isn't?" He sounded surprised.

Chelsea laughed. It wasn't exactly a stupid assumption on his part, considering she'd crept into his bedroom in the middle of the night. "No."

He made a sort of strangling sound, then said, "Let me guess—you came to ask for help with a crossword puzzle?"

She kissed him lightly on his lips. "I came to ask you again."

"Ask me what?" he demanded, sounding exasperated. "In my present state I'd roll on the floor and bark like a dog if you'd—"

"Remember what I asked you before? You said I should think it over for a while."

"Oh, that," Connor said, his voice suddenly serious.

Chelsea laced her fingers through his. "I . . . I can't stand worrying that you might get deported," she whispered.

"I don't love the idea myself," he said sarcastically.

"I'm serious, Connor. I don't want to lose you."

"I'm pretty quick on my feet," he reassured her.

Chelsea hesitated. Through the half-open window she could hear the steady lapping of the bay. "But we'll never be able to relax," she said at last. "It could happen any day, at any time."

"That's my life," Connor said quietly. "That's the truth of it."

"It doesn't have to be," Chelsea argued. "You know there's one way to make you legal."

"Chelsea—"

She kissed him again, quieting him, though her own heart was pounding. "I'm asking you, Connor. Will you marry me?"

"Isn't it traditional to get down on one knee?"

"I'm serious. Will you?"

Her words hung in the air. Connor stroked her cheek with the back of his hand. "It's not that simple," he said at last.

"Why not?"

Connor exhaled heavily. "First, because we barely know each other."

"I know enough," Chelsea pressed. "I know I love you."

"I have a bloody awful temper."

"I know."

"I snore."

"Believe me, I know. Don't forget, we share a very thin wall."

Connor looked away. "You've got a life to live, Chelsea," he said firmly. His voice had an edge to it now. "You're going to college. You're a talented artist. You've got a future all mapped out in front of you, plain as day." He paused. "I'll not be getting in the way of your plans."

"But you won't, Connor," Chelsea argued. "I can still go to college. You can come with me. You'd like New York. It's full of Irish people."

"And many of them illegal," Connor said darkly.

"But you won't be, not if we go through with this."

Connor didn't answer. He lay back, one arm behind his head, the rising and falling of his chest just visible in the ivory moonlight.

"It doesn't have to be like we're really married, Connor," Chelsea whispered. "If you're not ready to . . . you know, be with one person forever. I just want you to be safe."

"Chelsea Lennox, there's no woman I'd rather be with forever."

"Then will you stop being noble and answer me?" Chelsea demanded. "Will you marry me or not, you stubborn Irish jerk?"

For a long while Connor was silent. Then he grinned, shook his head, and kissed her hand. "Yes, Chelsea," he said, "I will."

Connor watched Chelsea leave, feeling an odd mixture of emotions, not one of which was pure and undiluted joy. He threw back the covers and fumbled in the dark for his bathrobe. It was a threadbare plaid rag, but it gave in all the right places.

It had been a long day, and he should have been able to fall straight back to sleep. But the brush with the Immigration cops had left his nerves badly frayed, and now Chelsea's sweet, decent offer was just making things worse. He didn't want to drag innocent people into his problems, especially not Chelsea, but it had been a close call that noon. A matter of seconds and inches.

Everyone at the job site had assured him that the Immies weren't usually this much trouble. After all, the nearest Immigration office was more than a hundred miles away. The belief seemed to be that a task force must have targeted Ocean City in hopes of making enough noise to keep at least some of the employers in line. Sooner or later, all the smart guys at the job said, the Immies would get tired of it and go on home.

Which didn't help him one damn bit if they caught him in the meantime. He'd be back on a plane to Ireland. To unemployment. To very little hope of a future.

And away from Chelsea, unless she came with him.

He grinned sourly. Somehow he couldn't quite picture her fitting in with Irish society. It wasn't that his people were particularly racist. It was just that they didn't have many black people in their town.

No, his family and friends would not get used to him having a black American girl on his arm. Ever. They'd be expecting him to go back to Molly.

He snapped on a shaded lamp with a low bulb and opened the drawer of his bedside table. He took out a letter, written on thin, blue-tinted paper. For a few moments he read it over, then refolded it and put it back in the drawer.

He grabbed a yellow pad and a pen. Then he sat on the bed and began to write.

Dear Molly,
   I got your letter five days after you sent it, which seems quick for a

cross-ocean trip. I tried to get in touch with you before I left for America, but your folks said you were away, visiting relatives all the way up in Sligo, although God only knows why you'd want to spend time *there*. They seemed leery of giving me your address and would only say that I could leave letters with them and they'd forward them on. It's not that I had anything in particular to write, it's only that I didn't want it to look like I had run out without so much as saying good-bye.

Connor read the letter back. It seemed to be opening with a lot of excuses. Well, that kind of made sense. His entire relationship with Molly had been full of excuses, his and hers.

I'm doing all right, living in a decent enough house and with a few friends. But things remain a bit uncertain. The American people are extremely friendly, but the American government officials are decidedly less so. I came within a few seconds of being snatched today and could be at almost any time.

The truth of what he had just written depressed him. At the same time there was something romantic about living a life on the edge. It added a certain desperate, Billy-the-Kid quality.

> Naturally I would love to see you again. It would be good to talk of old times and all we had between us.

There. Was that vague enough? He didn't want to blow her off, as the Americans said, because Molly was an unpredictable sort who, when insulted, might do any number of embarrassing things. Would she be angry at the past tense "had"? Well, if so, there was no helping it. One way or the other he had to deliver the message.

> Still and all, Molly, I don't think you should come to the States to see me. I can't get you work, and I can't put you up. Perhaps someday, down the road, after I've found a way to get my green card. But not now.

No, definitely not now. Not when he was in love with Chelsea and she apparently with him.

I'm sure, if you have bought a ticket, you can trade it in or sell it. That's what I strongly advise, anyway. Trust me when I say that there is no good for you in coming here.

None. And possibly plenty of harm to me, Connor thought grimly.

Now, how should he sign off? "Love, Connor"? "Yours truly"? How had she signed off?

He retrieved her letter and glanced at the end. "Love." All right, then, no point in seeming cold.

Then something caught his eye. A single word in the next-to-last sentence. "We hope to see you soon."

"We"? Since when had Molly started using the royal we?

three

The dials on Justin's clock showed 2:14 A.M. He felt his face and realized it was wet. Dog slobber.

"Oh, Mooch, *now?*" He groaned softly.

Mooch whimpered.

"All right," Justin whispered. He drew back the covers as quietly as he could. The sound of Kate's breathing changed in pitch, but she didn't awaken.

Justin fumbled in the dark for his denim cutoffs. Mooch whimpered again, trying to hurry him along.

"Come on," Justin said, leading the way down the rickety wooden steps. A dim night-light downstairs glinted off the chrome fittings on his boat, rocking gently between the catwalks.

"Justin?" Kate's sleepy voice floated down from the loft.

"I'm just taking Mooch out," Justin answered.

"Mmmm," Kate said.

"See," Justin reproached the dog. "You woke her up."

He opened the door, and Mooch beelined up to the bushes that surrounded the main house.

Justin stood on the pier, waiting patiently. There was a chill in the gentle breeze that wafted across the bay and tousled his hair. The moon shone down from a clear patch of sky fringed by swiftly moving gray-blue clouds. Stars blinked in and out.

The sound of water sloshing against the pilings had become so much a part of his life since moving into the boathouse that, like the slow creaking of weathered timbers and the lonely croaking of the resident frogs, he scarcely noticed it anymore.

The main house was dark, except for a low light shining from Connor's window on the south side. Even Grace's downstairs window was dark, and the shades were drawn. A good sign. It meant she was home, not in a bar or an alleyway, and at least contemplating sleep.

Mooch came back down the lawn, leaping joyfully.

"You done?" Justin asked. "Can we go back to bed now?"

But Mooch trotted down to the end of the pier and picked up his favorite piece of driftwood.

He carried it back to Justin, gazing up at him hopefully.

"Fetch? You think we're playing fetch at two in the morning? Are you nuts?"

Mooch, as usual, had no answer except to drop the driftwood at Justin's feet and yelp insistently.

"No way. It's sleep time. Kate's going to think I fell in."

But Mooch didn't move. He just pawed the driftwood. "You think that pathetic puppy-dog look is going to work on me?" Justin asked.

Then, snorting with annoyance, he reached down and picked up the stick, drew back, and hurled it toward the house. Mooch bounded after it.

Well, what the heck. He hadn't been paying as much attention to Mooch as he used to. Kate was taking up a bigger part of his life, and really, Mooch had been pretty gracious about accepting the way she took his place in the bed, relegating him to a well-chewed rug on the floor.

Mooch brought back the stick and laid it at Justin's feet again. "Okay, one more. That's it." Justin threw the stick, and Mooch took off.

Not as quickly as he had once done, Justin noticed. Mooch was getting on in years. He'd been Justin's dog for nine years, which made him at least ten. Pretty old in human years.

He'd wandered into Justin's life around the time his father had wandered out. A gaping hole had been filled by a big, shambling, always hungry, not very bright mutt.

Mooch brought back the stick, and Justin knelt to scratch him under the chin. "What do you think, pal? You like having Kate around? You think she's all right? You do? Me too." He grabbed Mooch's floppy ears and looked him in the eyes. "But you and me, we're still best buds, okay?"

The next morning, far too early for her taste, Grace Caywood trudged up the carpeted stairs to the top floor of The Claw, emerging beside the empty bar. Bright morning sunlight poured through the floor-to-ceiling windows in the dining room, fading into gloom before reaching the bar.

"Hi, Grace," Anton said softly. He was behind the bar, taking inventory on the beer in the cooler. He gave her a small, sad smile.

"Hi, Anton," Grace said, trying to keep the awkwardness out of her voice. "I, uh—" She winced, then exhaled slowly. "I hope I didn't get you in any trouble."

Anton shrugged. "Mike kept the whole thing from getting to Frank."

"He did?" Grace asked, surprised. So at least the restaurant's manager didn't know about what had happened. "That was nice of him."

"Mike's a good headwaiter. He looks out for his people." Anton smiled ruefully. "Besides, the last thing Mike wants is Frank on the warpath over employee drinking. He likes a shot himself now and then."

"Is he around? Mike, I mean."

"He's back in the office, putting together the shift schedule for next week. I'll get him for you."

Grace watched Anton disappear through the swinging doors into the brightly fluorescent kitchen. A moment later Mike appeared, carrying a clipboard. His expression was more regretful than angry. Anton emerged a moment later, avoiding her eyes.

"Grace," Mike said flatly.

"Hi, Mike."

"What's up?" he asked, sitting at the nearest bar stool.

Grace tried meeting his eyes and failed. This wasn't going to be easy. She wasn't used to asking for things. Especially not when she was so clearly the one in the wrong.

"I wanted to see if there was any chance you could put me back on the schedule," Grace said.

"I figured that was it." Mike stared past her out the windows. "Grace, you know I'm not a hard-ass, but you've been stealing drinks. Not one or two, but a lot. You were out of control."

Grace gritted her teeth. Any other time, any other circumstance, and she wouldn't have put up with being talked to this way. But she needed her job back.

She traced her finger along the smooth mahogany bar. "Yeah, I know I went a little too far," she admitted.

"You went far enough that you fell down carrying a tray full of food," Mike reminded her. "You were too drunk to walk."

"Look," Grace snapped, "I'm not running for the Mother Teresa award here. I'm not a saint, and neither are you. I'm hardly the only waiter here who drinks."

Mike raised his eyebrows. "Grace, I'm not so sure you're someone who has a drink only now and then."

"Meaning what?"

"Meaning I probably should have said something sooner. That wasn't the first time I saw you drunk on the job. It was just the worst." Mike sighed. "I think maybe you have a problem, Grace."

Grace clenched her fists. She wasn't sure

what she was, but she wasn't an alcoholic. Her mother was, not her.

"Go to hell, Mike," Grace muttered.

She started to turn away, but Mike reached for her arm. "Wait a minute."

"Why, you want to patronize me some more?"

Mike turned to Anton, who'd been hovering at a discreet distance. "Anton, pour me a scotch, straight up." He turned back to Grace. "We serve booze here, Grace. If you come back to work, then you'll have to serve it, be around it, smell it, know it's right there for the taking."

Anton set down a shot glass nearly filled with pale golden liquid. Mike slid the glass over to Grace.

Grace's eyes darted involuntarily to the glass for a moment. "What's this, some kind of test?"

"That's exactly what it is," Mike agreed.

Grace turned and looked at the glass. It was just a drink. It wasn't poison. It wasn't going to bite her. It was just a glass of scotch.

Like the glass Petie had put before her.

The ugly memory flooded back. A dark, empty bar. The hurricane's wind howling outside. She'd been too drunk to walk away but too thirsty to refuse the offer of that one drink.

Petie had reached for her blouse. She had

reached for the drink. She'd wanted to say no, but if she had, he would have taken away the drink. And she couldn't let that happen.

She'd said yes. She'd been willing to sell herself for a drink. He'd gaped at her, run his fat hands over her, kissed her with reeking breath and rough lips.

He'd passed out, drunker than she was, before he could take everything she was ready to give for another drink.

Grace tried to shake away the memory, taking a deep breath. She focused her gaze on the scotch. Her hand inched closer to it. She could smell it, peppery and sweet. She wanted it.

She looked over at Anton, cringing at the disappointment she could see in his eyes. Mike shook his head.

With an effort of will, Grace pulled her hand away. "I . . . ," she began, but her voice cracked. She bit her lip. "I can't come back to work yet, guys. Sorry."

Mike put his hand on her arm again. "Look, when you're really ready, you'll have a job here."

Grace forced a shaky smile and headed toward the stairs. They had been sweet, both of them. Nicer than she probably deserved. She felt like crying. But more than that, she felt like drinking.

four

Marta Salgado dipped a finger into her bathwater and swooshed it back and forth, adding to the small mountain of bubbles. She maneuvered her wheelchair closer to the edge of the tub, a move she liked to think of as parallel parking.

With strong arms Marta reached up and caught hold of the stainless-steel bar and pulley her father had installed over the tub. After all her years of practice since the shooting, getting into the tub was fairly easy.

The water was hot, very hot, but she didn't register the heat until her hips slid past the bubbles. She leaned back and sighed, savoring the warmth. With her legs hidden beneath the froth of bubbles like this, it was almost possible to forget how useless they were, how withered, how unlike the rest of her body.

She'd caught the look of shock and pity on Alec's face the first time she'd let him see them, that magical night when they'd gone swimming in a secluded, private lagoon. Still, a little pity was unavoidable. It had passed. And just as she hadn't missed that look, she also hadn't missed the way his hands had trembled when he'd touched her or the way he'd gulped nervously before he kissed her.

Marta washed carefully, then drained the water and levered herself forward to turn on the shower and rinse away the soap beneath the cool, invigorating spray.

Getting out of the tub was harder than getting in. She began by draping a terry-cloth robe across her wheelchair. She toweled off her hair, her shoulders, her chest. Then, with a herculean pull, she lifted and shoved herself back into the chair and finished toweling her lower body. She closed the robe around herself and went out into the hall, rolling the few feet to the kitchen.

"You want eggs?" her father asked, looking up from the Sunday newspaper. He looked as proper as ever in his white golf shirt and the red shorts of the Beach Patrol.

"Daddy, I've told you a million times, you don't have to wait for me to have breakfast."

"Who's waiting?" Mr. Salgado asked. "I like to have a little coffee before I eat." He gestured at the mug in front of him.

"You shouldn't eat so many eggs," Marta chided. "It's bad for you." She went to the refrigerator, opened it, and pulled out a half-full carton of eggs.

"Ha. My cholesterol is lower than yours," he said. He slapped his stomach. "And I'm in as good a shape as any of my lifeguards. I can still outswim and outrun any of them."

"Even Alec?" Marta asked. "He seems awfully strong to me."

Luis put down the paper and shook his finger at her. "Don't you start in with me. It's too early for me to be hearing about that pretty boy." He raised the paper again.

Marta grinned and placed a cast-iron frying pan on the burner. She could almost count the seconds before her father returned the paper to the table.

"Besides," her father said, "just because he looks like one of those underwear models doesn't mean he's a good lifeguard."

"Is he a good lifeguard?" Marta cracked four eggs in rapid succession.

Her father shrugged. "He's all right," he grumbled. "I suppose you're going out to see him after breakfast?"

"We're going to run some errands together. And then tonight I'm going over to his house to meet all his housemates." It should be no big deal meeting Alec's friends. She'd already met Kate, Chelsea, and Grace—although none of them knew she and Alec had been seeing each other almost every day.

But the thought of meeting Alec's male housemates—Justin and Connor—made her a little nervous. Would Alec be embarrassed to introduce her as his girlfriend? She knew guys could be pretty competitive about how good-looking their girlfriends were. And having a girlfriend in a wheelchair . . . oh, well. She'd never worried about that before. She wasn't about to start now.

"His house?" Her father looked at her, his forehead creasing in concern. "What for, dinner?"

"Poker, actually."

"Whatever happened to dinner and a movie?" Luis frowned. "I don't trust that boy."

"I love to play poker, Daddy," Marta said, keeping a watchful eye on her eggs. "And who taught me everything I know?"

"Take him for every penny he's got," Luis advised, scanning the sports page. "Which shouldn't be much, not with what we pay him."

"You know," Marta reflected, reaching for a spatula in the dishwasher, "it's lucky we can spend the day together. Alec used to have to work Sundays, and with me working at the clinic the rest of the week, he was afraid we'd never get a chance to see each other."

Luis grunted. "You see him plenty. The boy's trouble, if you ask me. He must call here twenty times a day."

Marta reached over and pushed down his newspaper, staring her father in the eyes. "Who makes out Alec's work schedule, you fake?"

Luis suppressed a grin. "You know, you need to learn more respect for your father. You're getting to be a rotten kid."

Marta gave him a kiss on the cheek. "Yeah, and you're a lousy father."

"You tell that boy, if he hurts you, I'll kill him."

Marta nodded solemnly. "He knows, Daddy. Like all your lifeguards, he lives in terror of you."

"In terror? Really?" Luis smiled broadly and nodded contentedly. "Now I know my life is a success."

Grace paused at the bottom of the open wooden stairs behind city hall. She'd promised David she'd come this evening, promised she'd give it a chance.

She trudged upstairs to the painted brown door. A sign there announced the evening's offerings: Codependents Support Group, 5 P.M. Adult Children of Alcoholics, 5 P.M. Alcoholics

Anonymous, 6 P.M. At the bottom of the sign some joker had taped a flyer from a nearby bar: Blue Monday Bikini 'n' Beer Bash.

Grace smiled grimly. A beer. That's what she really needed. But David would be waiting for her, and if she didn't show, there'd be the inevitable phone call, the "What are you afraid of?" The guilty recriminations. He wasn't pushing her too hard, not yet, but you could hear it in his voice—he'd seen the light, and he wanted her to convert, too. Maybe all ex-drunks were that way.

She hadn't been on a date with David since the bender that had finally convinced her she had a problem, the one that had sent her stumbling, horrified and desperate, into this place. They'd talked on the phone, about his drinking, about hers, but this would be their first encounter since that awful night. She'd suggested, only half joking, that they meet at a bar. David had countered with A.A. He'd won.

Grace didn't want to blow it with David. He mattered too much to her, enough even for her to put up with an hour of preaching from a bunch of loonies and losers.

The meeting room was full of metal folding chairs facing a small platform with a podium. Two dozen or so people milled around under a low ceiling of cigarette smoke. At least half the people there smoked, an edgy, chain-smoking cross section of humanity, black and white, young and old, male and female.

"Hi, Grace."

She turned to see David, looking as incredible as ever in deep blue jeans and his favorite leather jacket.

She nodded in acknowledgment. It was hard to know how to respond to him. She wanted him to touch her. She was afraid to touch him.

He stepped closer and looked her up and down, amusement in his dark eyes. "Kind of conservative for you, isn't it?"

Grace glanced down at her black cotton pants and white shirt. "Well, I . . ."

David laughed. "This isn't church," he said in a low voice. "At least, not exactly."

"Sorry. Emily Post doesn't say what to wear to an A.A. meeting. I thought I'd better go with the demure, repentant look."

"And not look too much like a drunk?"

He'd said it as a joke, but the words stung. "Former drunk," she said softly.

David gazed at her seriously. "The theory here is one day at a time, Grace. You may not buy the whole A.A. program, but I know that part's right."

"Don't start preaching at me, David," Grace

snapped. She cringed inside. "Look, it's just that I don't want you and me to be about drinking," she added in a softer tone. She paused. "Or about *not* drinking."

"You're right," David replied, shaking his head. "If I start doing that again, you can slap me."

He touched her shoulder, and she felt something relax inside her.

"So," David said. "When are you going to let me give you your next flying lesson?"

Grace felt her cheeks heat up. "I kind of don't have an income right at the moment."

"Your credit's good with me."

"I can't take—"

"Hey, I'm not kidding about it being credit," David protested. "I'll keep track. I'll charge interest, and if you don't pay me eventually, I'll hound you day and night. This isn't charity."

"David, David, haven't I told you about picking up on the new inmates?"

A girl with shoulder-length, wildly tangled hair appeared beside them. Her voice was loud and shrill. She was shorter than Grace, perhaps a little younger, and heavy. She wore a blue oxford shirt that pulled tight around her. Part of the tail hung out of her worn gray men's pants. Her round shoulders were hunched forward, but she moved with a certain smoothness and energy in spite of her size.

"Beth, this is Grace," David said. "And vice versa. And Beth," he pretended to chide, "you know how we frown on terms like 'inmates.'"

Beth glanced over her shoulder. "The sincerity cops aren't around," she began in a conspiratorial whisper. "Are they?" She paused, staring at Grace challengingly. "You don't remember me, do you?"

"Should I?"

Beth rolled her eyes. "No, I guess not. Of course, we went to school together, and it wasn't a very big school, but I'm not exactly surprised you don't remember me."

"You went to O.C. High?"

"I was a year behind you, but we were in some of the same classes."

"How could that be?" Grace asked.

Beth spread her chubby hands wide. "I'm one of those smart kids. You, on the other hand, were one of those cool kids, not that I'm accusing you of being in any way unintelligent."

Grace racked her brain, trying to conjure up a memory of Beth, but nothing came.

"Try pretending you remember me," Beth advised. She gripped Grace's arms with her fists. "Otherwise I may become depressed. Despondent. I may think my life is worthless." Her voice rose. "I may start drinking and not stop till I'm lying passed out in the surf and a bunch of ecology nuts mistake me for a beached whale and try to refloat me! Grace, don't let it happen!"

Grace recoiled in shock while David laughed. "Would you knock it off, Beth?" he said. "Grace is still getting adjusted to being surrounded by alcoholics. Let's not make her think she's fallen in with schizophrenics."

"Schizophrenics?" Beth arched an eyebrow at David. "That was an example of clinical paranoia, David, but certainly not outright schizophrenia. You know nothing about psychology."

Grace snapped her fingers. "Betty!" she said, the memory hitting her all at once. "You used to call yourself Betty, not Beth. Big—" She stopped herself, wishing she could call back the word.

"Big Betty," Beth said with only a trace of bitterness. "You do remember. I'm flattered. And you were Racey Gracie."

"Racey?" David repeated.

"Every boy's dream, every girl's ideal," Beth said.

At the podium a woman was urging everyone to their seats. Grace looked over at her, suddenly remembering why they were all here. "Yeah?" she muttered. "And now I'm just another drunk."

"Oh, sure," Beth said, laughing. "You got all

44

the best-looking guys at school, and now you waltz in and get the best-looking man in A.A. You're still the same old Racey."

An hour later Grace shifted her Eclipse into third gear and ripped down the main drag, weaving past a knot of cars, their drivers tourists, no doubt, meandering along with the usual lost look. The windows were down, and the warm night air whipped her dark hair around, stinging her forehead and cheeks. She caught David staring at her, grinning widely.

"You know, you ought to be a pilot," he said. "You drive like a pilot."

"Is that a compliment?" she asked.

"Not necessarily. All the guys in my squadron used to own hot sports cars. Fighter jocks think they can drive anything at any speed."

She glanced over at him. "But you were too mature for all that, I suppose."

"Absolutely. My car was a nice sedate Toyota." He winced as she raced a yellow light. "Of course," he added, "my Harley could blow all their cars away and did on several occasions."

"Hey, when are you going to take me for a ride?" Grace asked.

David grinned. "That sounded wonderfully suggestive."

Grace felt her neck muscles tense. "No, I didn't mean it that way," she said quickly. David looked surprised and a little hurt, and she realized how cold she must have sounded.

"Sorry. I . . ." Grace sighed, feeling a quivery edge in her throat. "I'm just in a bitchy mood, I guess. I think Beth got on my nerves."

"I like her," David said. "I guess she takes some getting used to, though."

For a while they drove on in silence. The town had the usual subdued, Sunday-night feel, but the miniature golf course was doing great business, and most of the restaurant parking lots were full. The traffic was bad, too. Grace had to go all the way to the north end to pick up her younger brother. He'd promised to be waiting out in front of the condo, sparing her the sight of their mother.

"You know, David, you don't really have to go to this dumb poker game if you don't want to," Grace said, breaking the silence. "I mean, if you're just doing it to be nice."

"Nice, hell. I like to play cards. Besides, it will give me a chance to get to know your friends and your little brother better." He thought for a moment. "Does that bother you? I mean, is it like I'm moving in on you too fast?"

Grace changed to the far right lane and slowed the car down to something more or less approaching the speed limit. "No, that's not it at all. You're the best thing in my life," she said. "It's . . . look, David, something kind of happened while I was . . . you know."

"Drinking."

"Stinking, puking drunk," Grace said under her breath.

"And?"

"And, well, it's nothing, really. No biggie. It's just kind of that the whole thing has me feeling weird and off center."

"What happened?"

Grace started to explain, but a knot formed in her throat. She swallowed with difficulty and fought to keep tears out of her eyes. She tried again to speak but found she couldn't.

David nodded. "I understand, Grace. When you're ready, I'll be here."

Grace smiled shakily and pointed to the street corner up ahead. "There's Bo."

five

"Cards?" Justin asked.

"Three decks," Alec confirmed. Of course, one of those decks was missing the four of diamonds.

"Chips?"

"For eating or for playing?"

"Both."

"Got 'em," Alec said.

"Dip?"

"Onion and bean," Alec said, pointing to two open plastic tubs on the dining-room table.

"What do we have to drink?" Justin asked.

Alec counted off on his fingers. "Coke, iced tea, that jug of pink stuff, and Connor says he'll share his beer, only it's that lousy dark stuff he keeps at room temperature, so forget that."

Justin looked uncomfortable. "Should we have beer? I mean, David's coming straight from an A.A. meeting with Grace."

Alec shrugged. "I don't know. What's the protocol on these things?"

Kate and Chelsea came in from the kitchen. Kate was wearing a pair of ultrashort shorts that showed off her tan legs. Alec winced. Would Marta be bothered by that? "I don't think Grace or David would want us treating them like cripples," Kate said as she grabbed a handful of potato chips.

Alec winced again.

"Yeah, but they are, in a way," Justin observed. "Grace is just starting to get her act under control a little."

"Well, it's Connor's beer," Alec said. He tossed a chip at Mooch, who caught it midflight. "Maybe we should just leave it up to him." Another household debate over beer was the last thing he wanted to get into. He had other concerns. Maybe he should have warned everyone. Maybe he shouldn't have left it to be a big surprise. But really, what was the alternative? Make a big issue out of the fact that his girlfriend was in a wheelchair?

"Leave it up to Connor?" Kate was saying. "Oh, by all means, trust Connor's delicate sensibilities."

"I heard that," Connor called from the living-room couch. He stood, stretched, and came over to inspect the dining-room table. "Now, personally, I don't drink when I'm gambling," he said, curling his lip at the bean dip. "Especially when it's such a new game as poker is to me."

Justin cocked his eyebrow and shot Alec a look. "You haven't played much poker?"

"No," Connor answered, a sound that came out "noo." "I thought maybe you fellows would teach me."

"Sure, we'll teach you," Justin said.

"Glad to," Alec agreed. "Our pleasure."

"So where are the rest of our players?" Justin wondered aloud. "I guess David and Grace are picking up Bo on the way. Am I forgetting someone?"

Alec realized he might as well get this over with. It wasn't like anyone would *say* anything rude. "Uh, yeah," he admitted hesitantly. "I invited a friend of mine."

"Who? Is it someone we know, and does he have money?" Justin prodded. "Answer that last question first."

Alec swallowed. "Actually, it's a girl."

"Ahhh," Chelsea said. "'It's a girl,' he says casually, as if we wouldn't possibly be interested."

"Well, I guess that clears up the question of whether you're interested in girls at all," Connor said slyly. "And me keeping my bedroom door locked at night."

"Connor, don't be a jerk," Chelsea said.

"Yes, dear," Connor answered meekly.

"So, are you going to tell us who—" Justin began, just as there was a noise at the front door. Alec jumped nervously. He trotted quickly toward the door, but it opened before he got there. Grace held it open while David pulled Marta's wheelchair up the stairs. Bo was bringing up the rear.

Alec rushed out to help David clear the final step.

"Thanks for the lift," Marta said casually to David. She gave Alec a wink.

Alec felt the familiar softening he always felt when he saw her. She looked beautiful. Anyone would think that, wheelchair or not. And if they didn't, then they were just blind.

She was gorgeous, and smart, and strong, and funny. And best of all, she was his.

Justin held his breath, surprised, then instantly felt ashamed of himself for being shocked. So Alec's friend was in a wheelchair. No big deal. At least it shouldn't be. Besides, she was probably just a *friend* friend. No point in jumping to conclusions.

The girl rolled forward, tilting back expertly to clear her front wheels over the raised threshold.

Alec seemed to hesitate, then leaned down and kissed Marta lightly. On the lips. *Not* on the cheek. So much for her being just a *friend* friend.

Alec stood up and turned back to the rest

of the group. "Everyone, this is Marta Salgado."

"Hi, Marta," Kate said with a casual, familiar wave.

"Hi, Kate," Marta answered, grinning. When she smiled, Justin noticed, her wheelchair seemed to evaporate, and all you saw was that incredible face.

Marta turned her gaze on Chelsea. "Chelsea, how are you?"

"You know each other?" Alec asked.

"We sort of met at the clinic," Kate admitted.

Chelsea grinned. "Kate went there for unspecified reasons that we won't go into because it might be very embarrassing."

"Very cute, Chelsea," Kate cried, giving her friend a playful shove.

"Anyway," Alec said, "I guess you met David coming in, that's Justin, and that's Connor." He gave Marta a meaningful look. "Connor says he doesn't know how to play poker very well."

Marta's eyes lit up. "Doesn't he? Then we'd better get the game started."

"Salgado," Justin repeated slowly, the possibility beginning to dawn on him. "You know, our boss's last name is Salgado. You know him? Luis Salgado?"

"I know him vaguely," Marta said. "He's my dad."

Justin suppressed a grin. "Jeez, Alec. You're

going out with Luis's daughter? You're crazier than I thought."

Justin noticed Bo standing by himself in a corner, trying to catch his eye. "What's up, man?" he asked. Bo said nothing but slid around the corner in the direction of the kitchen.

"Everyone help yourself to whatever," Justin said, waving in the general direction of the food. "I'll grab the liquids out of the kitchen."

The kitchen was relatively clean, mostly because Kate and Grace insisted on it. There were two refrigerators, side by side, and a stove that was very nearly a genuine antique—not that anyone in the house used it much. What little cooking was done usually occurred in the microwave Kate had bought secondhand. Most of their diet was delivered in flat cardboard boxes.

"I gather you wanted to talk to me?" Justin said to Bo.

"Yeah. Did you know that Gracie was at an Alcoholics Anonymous meeting tonight?"

"Yep, I knew." He waited, but Bo just leaned against the kitchen counter and stared into space. "What's the matter?"

"What do you think? I mean, I knew my mom was a drunk, but I thought I could count on Gracie, at least."

Justin hesitated. "Look, she's trying to do something about it before it gets any worse."

"That's not what's bugging me," Bo admitted, glancing nervously toward the dining room. "It's just, well, first my mom, now my sister. Does that mean I'm next?"

Justin almost laughed, then realized it wasn't an entirely stupid question. "I'm not exactly an expert on this stuff, Bo," he said, "but I don't think anyone's really totally sure whether alcoholism is passed on through your genes or if it's something you just learn. I can see what you mean, though. It seems like either way, you're gonna have to be careful."

"It isn't fair," Bo protested.

Justin smiled wryly. "I don't see much point in spending your time worrying about whether you'll turn out to be an alcoholic, too, Bo. Your dad doesn't drink, does he?"

Bo shook his head. "I don't think so. But it's not like I can really be sure, not with him off in California. Still, he left because he couldn't handle Mom's drinking, so I guess he's not a drunk."

"There you go," Justin said. "Figure you'll end up like your dad instead of your mom. Also, keep an eye on yourself down the road. If you start to like it too much, quit right then."

Bo didn't look convinced. "You know, you're supposed to be older and wiser than me, Justin. My male role model and all. But that's a pretty lame answer."

"Hey, I gave it my best shot, you ungrateful punk," Justin said, rapping him playfully on the head. "Go ask David if you want a better answer. He's got more experience with this than I do."

"No way," Bo said with a knowing laugh. "He's all in love with Grace and everything. You're over her, at least most of the way, so I can get a straight answer from you."

Justin loaded up with lemonade and sodas from the refrigerators and handed some to Bo to carry. Then he pushed open the kitchen door and rejoined the crowd. Marta, Alec, and Connor were already seated at the table, passing around the chips and dip. Kate and Chelsea were getting ready to take off to a movie with Grace, and David was kissing Grace good-bye. Not a major kiss, Justin noted. Maybe ten percent more than what Alec had given Marta.

"*There* you are," Alec said. "Where did you go? Someone just called for you. I yelled, but you didn't answer."

"Who called?"

Alec shrugged. "Don't know. Some guy. Said he didn't want to leave a message." Alec reached for a deck of cards. "He asked if I knew what your middle name was. Some jerk who thinks he's funny."

*   *   *

The next morning Grace walked toward the kitchen through a disaster area. A deck of cards seemed to have been tossed across the living room. Crusty bowls of bean dip decorated the dining-room table. And the pathetic attempt the guys had made to clean up had resulted in a pile of dirty dishes in the kitchen sink.

Great. Well, they could clean it up when they got home from work. Just because she was temporarily out of work herself didn't mean she was the maid.

On the other hand, she had no plans for the day aside from moping around the house, and that would be more tolerable if it were clean.

Grace carved out a path to the faucet and filled the coffee machine. While she waited for the coffee to brew, Grace turned on the little black-and-white TV that Alec had brought from home. Oprah was doing a show on teen alcoholics. An overweight girl with bad teeth was sobbing into a tissue about her battle with the bottle. Grace thought of Beth and turned off the TV.

She was nothing like Beth or those red-eyed, repentant kids on *Oprah*. The A.A. meeting last night had meant nothing to her. The punch was bad, the cookies were stale, and so was the propaganda. "One day at a time"—now, *there* was an original thought.

Although she would have suffered through

a meeting of the Ocean City zoning commission if it had meant she could see David again. She'd felt awkward with him, not at all her usual confident self. But when he'd kissed her good-bye at the end of the night, none of that seemed to matter. It was as if he were a link to some lost, better part of herself.

While the coffee machine burbled, Grace scraped encrusted food off the plates in the sink. Guys were such slobs.

She had just extracted an ace of spades from the onion dip when the phone rang. She ran to the hallway to grab it, her fingers covered with goop. "Yes?" she said, a hint of irritation in her voice.

"May I speak to either Chelsea Lennox or Connor Riordan, please?"

Grace frowned. She knew that voice, but from where? "They're not home. Who's this?" she asked.

"I'll try them later," the girl said.

"Marta? Is that you, Marta?"

"Hi, Grace," Marta said after a moment of silence.

"Hi, what's up?" Why did Marta sound so weird? Very formal and unlike her usual self. "You want me to leave Chelsea a message?"

"Is she already at work?" Marta asked, evading Grace's question.

"Chelsea? Yeah, she's down at the beach. Are you at the clinic? You could probably see her walking past on the boardwalk if you wait long enough."

"Yes, I'm at the clinic," Marta said, her words clipped.

"Marta, do you have a message or not?" Grace asked, annoyed at the mysterious tone of the whole conversation.

"Um, well, Chelsea and Connor have an appointment with us for today at noon, and we want to reschedule it. Our lab guy—" Marta cut herself off. "Um, if you run into Chelsea, tell her five this afternoon would be better for us."

Grace laughed. "So Chelsea's finally made the big birth-control appointment, huh?" She paused, frowning. "But what do you need the lab for?"

Marta sighed heavily. "Grace, this is kind of a personal matter, all right? Just forget I called. If Chelsea or Connor comes home . . . no, forget it. Forget the whole thing. Bye."

Grace stared at the receiver as the dial tone buzzed in her ear. "Now, what was that all about?" she muttered.

six

Justin and Alec paused in front of Floaters, breathing in the aroma of greasy burgers. "Where are you going?" Justin asked when Alec kept on walking.

Alec shrugged. "I'm going to run down and say hi to Marta at the clinic."

Justin shook his head. "You're giving up lunch?"

"I thought maybe I'd catch something down there with her. You know, sort of a surprise."

"You should be careful about surprises," Justin warned. "What if she's having lunch with some other guy and you walk in?"

Alec shook his head. "That's one thing I don't worry about with Marta."

"I wouldn't be too sure. You know, if I didn't have Kate . . ." Justin let the implication hang provocatively.

Alec laughed easily and glanced down the boardwalk in the direction of the clinic.

"She's got you in the palm of her hand, Daniels," Justin teased. "It's mighty pathetic to see."

He watched for a moment as Alec plunged into the teeming boardwalk crowd, disappearing in a sea of white legs and sunburned bald heads.

The sun was fierce today, so hot that it seemed a few more degrees would turn the sandy beach to glass. The vendors who rented out beach umbrellas were doing a good business as the older tourists sought shelter. Even the water looked hot, sloshing sullenly against the shore and glittering lazily.

Justin stepped into the dark, cool interior of Floaters. It was a hangout for lifeguards and other boardwalk regulars and managed to convey an air of detachment that scared off outsiders. He searched the scarred wooden tables for a vacant seat and finally located a face he knew, another lifeguard he was on hi-how-are-you? terms with.

"Hey, Boyles." Justin slid into the seat across from him.

"Garrett." Steve Boyles nodded, looking pretty hung over. He was halfway through a crab-cake sandwich.

"You're a brave man, eating crab cakes here," Justin said, casting a suspicious glance at the sandwich. "I think those are left over from the early nineties."

"Thanks, Garrett, just what my stomach needs."

"Burger, medium rare, fries, and a chocolate shake," Justin instructed the waitress.

Steve grinned. "Like they know medium rare from burned to a crisp."

"I keep hoping," Justin said. "Who knows, someday they may hire a real cook instead of whoever's on the work-release program from prison."

Steve laughed. "You still living in the house o' babes?" he asked.

Justin nodded.

"So when are you going to invite me over, or are you saving them all for yourself?"

"They're all pretty much hooked up with someone right now," Justin said. "I didn't realize you were having trouble meeting women."

"I'd like to meet that Grace chick I saw over by your chair last week."

"She's involved."

"But not with me," Steve argued, "which means she hasn't experienced a real man."

Justin took the milk shake the waitress brought him and slurped down a big swallow. "She's into a guy who's twenty-six, owns his own plane, and used to be a fighter pilot."

Steve made a pained face. "Oh, hurt me."

"I hear he was in Desert Storm and shot down an Iraqi MiG," Justin added, enjoying the crumpled look on the other lifeguard's face.

The burger arrived, and Justin bit into it hungrily. Someday he was going to have to start worrying about what he ate, but not today.

He noticed Steve staring past him toward the boardwalk. "What, you see the new girl of your dreams?" Justin asked.

"Not exactly," Steve said. "Some guy keeps staring in here. Either at me or at you, and I'd rather believe it's you."

Justin glanced over his shoulder. The usual boardwalk parade passed by in both directions. Only one person wasn't moving, a slim, middle-aged man who was standing still and clearly staring into the restaurant. He did seem to be staring at Justin, and he turned away quickly when Justin met his shaded gaze.

"Friend of yours?" Steve asked.

Justin shrugged. "Don't think so." But Justin realized he had seen the man before. When? Here, on the beach, or at some other time, some other place?

"I guess it's not just the women who go for you, you man, you," Steve continued.

"Now what makes you think the guy was gay?" Justin snapped.

"Give me a break. The guy was definitely not straight."

Justin sighed. "I wish I had your amazing ability to read minds that way."

"So if that wasn't it, why was he staring at you?"

Justin shrugged again, feeling troubled, but not quite sure why.

Chelsea stood back with Connor while Marta maneuvered her chair into the tiny, stuffy room. Then she sat in one of the two molded-plastic chairs while Connor flopped down beside her.

Connor wiped his brow. "It's hot enough to roast out there."

"It's brutal," Chelsea agreed. "I can't even sell any pictures. Everyone I go up to asks me if I'm selling drinks. I could push lemonade at ten bucks a glass out on that beach today."

Marta leaned forward and rested her elbows on the tiny desk that separated her from the two of them. "Look, I might as well get this out right away. First of all, our lab guy is out till late this afternoon, so we can't do the blood test until then."

Connor groaned. "I could have been hanging out in the shade," he said.

"Wait, there's more," Marta said. "I called your house to tell you, and I got Grace. She recognized my voice."

Chelsea started. "Grace knows?"

"I didn't give her any details, but she knows you and Connor were coming in today at noon for something that would involve lab work."

This time it was Chelsea's turn to groan. "Oh no." What would Grace think was going on?

"I doubt Grace would say anything to anyone," Connor pointed out. "She's got her own secrets."

Chelsea buried her face in her hands. "This town!" she said through her fingers. She looked back up at them. "A quarter million people on a sunny day, yet it's still a small town where everyone learns everyone else's business!"

"Sorry," Marta said.

"It's not your fault," Chelsea said. "I just don't want Kate finding out about this too soon. She'll start in on me with the whole do-you-really-think-this-is-the-right-thing? routine."

Connor slapped the desktop briskly. "Well, there's no point in worrying about it when there's nothing we can do. Let's go and grab a quick lunch. Marta, we'll see you at five, then." He stood up and pulled Chelsea to her feet.

"Grace will probably stay quiet," Chelsea reassured herself.

Connor reached for the door. "Besides, all she can do is guess. There must be tons of perfectly simple reasons why we'd both be stopping by the clinic." He pulled the door open. "A premarital blood test is probably the last thing she'd—"

He stopped in midsentence.

Chelsea looked past him and saw Alec. She threw up her hands. "Oh, great."

"What are you guys doing here?" Alec asked.

"What are *you* doing here?" Marta asked in exasperation.

"I just came to see if you wanted to go have lunch." Alec smiled reluctantly at Connor and Chelsea. "We could all go together."

"Wonderful," Chelsea said bleakly. "Then we could invite Kate and my brother and my parents and the local TV station."

"We don't want this to get around," Connor told Alec, his tone firm.

"Want what to get around?" Alec asked innocently.

Connor's expression relaxed into a smile. He glanced at Chelsea. "Nothing. We just stopped by to say hi to Marta."

Chelsea nodded vigorously. "Right."

"Well, thanks for stopping by, you two," Marta said.

Chelsea flashed her a grateful smile. "Bye," she said, pulling Connor along with her.

Out on the boardwalk again, Chelsea breathed a sigh. "So, do you think Alec heard?"

Connor shook his head. "No. As usual, the boy wonder was oblivious."

"I guess we'll know soon enough," Chelsea said. "The first sign will be the eruption of Mount Kate."

"So what did you hear?" Marta asked Alec.

Alec laughed and bent down to kiss her. "I heard 'premarital blood test.'"

"Grace knows, too," Marta said. "Thanks to my brilliance. But Kate's not supposed to know. Chelsea's afraid she'll try to talk her out of it." *Not that talking Chelsea out of it would be a bad idea*, she added silently.

"Marriage." Alec shivered.

Marta made an expressive shoving-away gesture. "Not my concern. Clinic business is supposed to be confidential, and no one is asking my opinion." She shot Alec an annoyed look. "You might try calling before you just show up, Alec."

"Why, because you might have been having lunch with another guy?" Alec chuckled.

"What if I were?" Marta demanded.

Alec's eyes widened in surprise—then the

smug smile returned. "I'd get rid of him."

"Really. I'm glad to see you're so confident," Marta said. "You should keep an eye on that ego. It might just become too big for you to contain."

Later that evening Kate leaned against the loft railing as she stared down at Justin's boat, wedged between the two catwalks, its prow facing the open, barnlike doors. Beyond, in the still-bright water, windsurfers tried in vain to ride the afternoon's hot, fitful breeze. The sun's rays were low on the horizon, sending shafts of light directly into the cool gloom of the boathouse.

Justin sat up into a dusty golden beam that turned his strong, tan shoulders red and lit highlights in his dark hair. He sent her a lazy, contented grin as he climbed out of the bed.

Kate crossed to the chair where she had hurriedly thrown her clothing and began to dress, playfully evading his grasp.

"So, I kind of forgot to ask," he said, scrounging around for his own shorts. "How was work?"

She shrugged. "I spent the whole day cataloging slides. Cross sections of shark liver."

"Sounds like fun," he said.

"It's kind of a sign of Shelby's confidence in

me. It means she trusts me to do more than just feed the fish and mop up." Kate pulled on her top. The liver had come from a shark that had washed up dead on a beach just a few hundred yards from the Safe Seas Institute, where she worked. Shelby was looking for evidence of disease in the shark—a mostly lost cause since sharks basically never get sick. "It's boring, but it's an honor, if you know what I mean."

"Hmmm," Justin responded vaguely. He seemed to be arguing with himself over something.

"What?" she pressed.

"Look, Kate. What if a guy had this secret, and it kind of involved his girlfriend, only someone else had told him not to tell her?"

Kate felt her heart race. Secret? She bit her lip, glancing at Justin. "I guess that would depend on what the secret was," she said, trying to keep her voice level. "If, say, it was a guy keeping something from his girlfriend that she ought to know, I guess he should just tell and get it over with because she'd find out sooner or later."

Justin stared at her for a moment, frowning in confusion—then a light seemed to dawn in his eyes. He grinned. "No, it's not *that* kind of secret." He rolled his eyes. "Where would I get the energy to be running around with another girl?"

Kate let out a deep breath in relief. "Then what's the secret?" she asked.

"I can't say."

"Then why did you bring it up?"

"Because sooner or later you're going to find out, and you'll probably find out that I knew about it, and I don't want you pissed at me for not telling."

"But you're *not* telling," Kate pointed out.

"I'll tell you . . . in time. If you don't find out on your own." He grinned. "In the meantime I kind of told you, without actually telling you."

Kate sighed. "You can be very annoying sometimes, you know."

"Annoying is my middle name." He patted his stomach. "Also, starving is my middle name. Want to go up to the house and see if anyone else is interested in ordering a pizza?"

"Good idea," Kate said as she finished buttoning her shirt.

Justin wrapped his muscular arms around her waist, pulling her close. "Nice shirt. How about if I just unbutton it again?" he teased.

Kate tilted her head up to give him a light kiss. "I thought you were hungry."

"I am."

"You're always hungry," Kate said. She took his hand and led him toward the stairs. "Pizza. Try to think pizza."

Justin let himself be led. Mooch got slowly to his feet, looking quizzically at his master.

"Pizza," Justin told the dog. Mooch began to wag his tail and fell into step behind them. "Mooch likes Canadian bacon on his," Justin said.

Justin and Kate stepped out onto the pier, hand in hand. Suddenly Justin stopped, staring over at the house. Kate followed the direction of his gaze and felt a shiver run down her spine.

A man stood on the porch, staring right at them.

seven

"That guy," Justin said. "He was watching me today."

Justin kept walking, vaguely aware of Kate by his side as he kept his eye on the stranger standing on the porch. The man still wore the shades and the Dodgers hat he had worn when Justin had seen him at Floaters.

And at the beach. The memory came back suddenly. The day he and Alec had dealt with those two French girls. The man had been there, too. Watching.

Justin reached the foot of the stairs. "Can I help you?" he asked, his eyes narrowing in suspicion.

"Are you Justin Garrett?" The man's voice made Justin's whole body go cold.

"Yes."

The man pulled off his cap, revealing thinning dark hair. He slowly removed his sunglasses and focused his gaze on Justin. Justin felt his heart stop. His foot, raised to take the first step on the porch, came down hard. He stumbled and felt Kate reach for his arm.

"It's been so long, I wasn't sure. Justin. It's me," the man said softly. "Your father."

Justin stood absolutely still. Somewhere, far away, he could hear the high-pitched whine of a Jet Ski. He smelled barbecue smoke drifting from a nearby backyard. He heard a feminine giggle from inside the house. He saw his own long shadow, cast by the dying sun.

Some part of him said that he should feel . . . something. But he didn't feel a thing. He registered only disconnected, meaningless incidents all around him. He couldn't see the man on the porch. That man had slipped into a blind spot where Justin's eyes would not focus.

"Son . . . ," the man said uncertainly. And at the sound of that word, Justin's mind snapped back.

"Don't call me that," he cried in a voice he had never heard before.

"Justin, I wanted to see you."

"I don't want to see you."

The man stepped closer. He held out his hand.

Justin stepped up, brushing past him without another word, and went inside.

He heard a voice from behind him, floating through an open window. "Tell him I'm staying at the Ocean City Grand. I'll try him another time."

"All right," Kate answered neutrally.

A moment later she came through the door. "He's gone," she said.

Justin took a deep, shaky breath of air. It seemed thick and charged with electricity. "Good."

"He's staying in town," Kate said.

Justin shook his head slowly. "I don't care. If he calls, I'm not here. If he stops by again, I'm out. He'll give up eventually. He's good at that."

"Justin—" Kate began, reaching for him.

"No," Justin said. "Don't plead his case. I know all the arguments. He walked out, and now he wants to walk back in. He's sorry. Maybe he's lonely. Maybe he's curious about how I turned out. Maybe he wants to make up and start over again. I don't care. Just don't be on his side, Kate."

Kate withdrew her hand. "I didn't know there were sides."

"There are," Justin said harshly.

Kate nodded. "Then I'm on yours."

Suddenly Justin felt exhausted. A terrible weariness swept over him. He wanted to throw himself down on the couch and not think or feel or talk. Instead he forced a tight grin onto his face. "I'm still hungry. Let's see who's up for pizza."

"This is good pizza," Justin said enthusiastically. "Great. Much better than usual. More pepperoni. Is this the usual stuff? I mean, did we order this from the same place?"

Chelsea cast him a quick glance. When had Justin ever been this enthusiastic about pizza? Rapidly cooling pizza at that. He was definitely acting strange. What if he knew about the marriage plan? Or was she just being paranoid?

"This one is good, too," Kate chimed in, indicating the veggie pizza she and Chelsea and Alec were sharing. "Excellent."

Okay, now both of them were going on about the pizza. Kate didn't even particularly *like* pizza. Suddenly it was the center of her existence.

Chelsea glanced at Grace. Her face was strained. Her eyes kept darting toward Connor, who was drinking a dark brown Guinness from a glass. Was it the beer she was staring at? Or was Grace having a hard time keeping her mouth shut about Marta's phone call?

"What do you guys think about Marta?" Alec asked suddenly. He'd barely spoken till that moment.

"She's great," Justin said firmly. "Smart,

pretty, tough. And she can play poker, too."

"I really liked her," Kate agreed.

Alec frowned, as if he didn't like the answers. He turned his gaze on Connor. "You think she's—"

"I only met her at the poker game!" Connor blurted. He sent Alec a warning look.

Wonderful, Connor, Chelsea thought. *Very cool.*

"That's what I meant," Alec said, looking confused. Then his expression cleared. "Yeah. At the *poker* game. What did you think of her?"

"She's quite a girl," Connor said, his face beginning to redden. "I . . . I'd give her a tumble myself."

"You'd what?" Alec asked, his eyes flashing.

"Excuse me?" Chelsea snapped.

Connor took a long swig of his beer. "I *meant,* if I wasn't so mad about you, of course, Chelsea," he said. Then he turned to Alec. "And if Marta wasn't seeing you, also of course."

Chelsea sneaked another look at Grace, who was biting her fingernail, staring intently either at Connor or at Connor's beer.

"Great pizza," Justin said again, lifting another piece out of the box.

"We know!" Grace said. Her own slice was barely touched.

"I like it, too," Kate added, as if she were coming to Justin's rescue.

"Who cares? It's pizza, damn it," Grace exploded. She reached for her own soda and took a shallow swig.

For a moment no one spoke.

"Hot in here, isn't it?" Connor remarked.

"Why don't you take off your jacket if you're hot?" Kate suggested.

She knows about the blood tests, Chelsea thought desperately. *She knows, and she's just toying with us.*

Connor shook his head. "I like my jacket."

"Everyone likes every damn thing tonight," Grace said.

"You said you were hot," Kate persisted.

"I can decide whether or not to wear my bloody jacket, can't I?" Connor asked shrilly.

"When do you know when it's time to start, you know, getting serious, or exclusive, or whatever you want to call it?" Alec asked, as if he were in another universe. "And do you have to make it formal? I mean, shouldn't the girl just know?"

"Maybe it's the pepperoni, Connor," Kate said. "Spicy food can make you hot."

Chelsea let her forehead sink onto her crossed hands. "Just take the jacket off, Connor," she muttered. It was attracting too much attention now. Now that he'd opened his mouth about being hot.

"Chelsea," he said, giving her a look.

"Maybe it's the beer," Grace said. She laughed dryly. "Alcohol makes you hot. I know it always did with me." She tried out her tense, mirthless laugh again.

I'm caught in the twilight zone, Chelsea thought as she raised her head. "Connor," she said. "Give it up. It's impossible to keep a secret in this house."

"Who's keeping secrets?" Justin snapped suddenly. "Maybe it's just none of your business."

"What?" Chelsea said.

"Justin—" Kate warned.

"If I wanted to go into it, I would, all right? I don't." Justin reached for another slice of pizza, then threw it back down into the box.

"If *you* wanted to go into it?" Chelsea asked.

"Justin," Kate said, "I don't think anyone even knows about that, so chill. I think this is about that other thing."

Justin's angry brow eased. "Oh. Jeez, sorry. Forget it. Sorry."

"You actually *told*, Grace?" Chelsea demanded, sending Grace a disappointed glare.

"You told Kate?" Alec demanded of Justin.

"Told who what?" Grace asked.

"Oh, so you *did* overhear, didn't you, Alec?" Chelsea said.

"I didn't tell her," Justin grumbled. "I just told her I *couldn't* tell her."

"Great," Alec moaned. "Don't tell Marta. She'll kill me."

"I told you he knew," Connor said to Chelsea. He started to pull off his jacket. "Either he heard, or Marta told him outright."

"What are you people babbling about?" Grace yelled.

Chelsea saw Kate's eyes focused on the reddish bruise in the crook of Connor's elbow.

"Oh," Grace said. "The lab-test thing. Of course I didn't tell anyone, Chelsea. Give me some credit. I can keep a secret."

Chelsea watched Kate absorb this last bit of information as her eyes traveled back to the red needle mark on Connor's arm. Chelsea could almost hear the wheels turning in her friend's head.

Kate turned a suspicious stare on Chelsea. "Lab tests? You and Connor are getting lab tests? Why?" Suddenly Kate's eyes widened dramatically. "Are you nuts?" she demanded.

Chelsea closed her eyes, listening to the sudden silence that descended over the group. Well, it had to come out sooner or later. It was going to be sooner. She stood up, sighed, and cleared her throat.

"In case anyone in this room still doesn't know, and I can see that everyone does know, Connor and I are getting married."

"Are you out of your mind?" Kate exploded as soon as she and Chelsea were out of the house.

Chelsea kept walking at a rapid pace, heading down the street in the direction of the boardwalk.

"I'm asking you, as your best friend, are you nuts?" Kate repeated.

"I'm not nuts," Chelsea replied.

"Are you pregnant or something?"

Chelsea stopped and rounded on Kate. "You know better than that."

"How would I know? Ten minutes ago I would have sworn you weren't dumb enough to even think about getting married," Kate cried. "Maybe I don't really know you at all."

They waited impatiently for a red light to change so they could cross the main boulevard, Chelsea silent and stoic, Kate pacing back and forth.

"Look, I'm just trying to understand, Chels," Kate said, trying to cool things down.

"Really? Sounded to me like you'd already made up your mind."

Kate opened her mouth to fire back a retort but thought better of it. She was never going to get anywhere if Chelsea stayed this defensive.

The light changed, and Kate followed Chelsea across. Four guys in a blue convertible whistled their appreciation.

"Chelsea, where are we going?" Kate asked. "Can't we sit down somewhere and talk for a little while about this?"

"I'm going to the beach. I want to see the ocean."

"You work on the beach. You see the ocean all day."

"Oh, but never as an engaged person! The whole world will look different now that I'm engaged, right? I mean, *you're* certainly treating me differently."

They climbed the wooden steps up to the boardwalk. The sky over the ocean was already dimming, the horizon indistinct and hazy. The bright neon of the boardwalk was flickering to life, and the crowds had shifted from bathing suits to T-shirts and shorts.

Chelsea put her hands on her hips and stared at the water. "Yep. There's the ocean." Then she turned right and headed down the boardwalk, ignoring Kate entirely.

"Chelsea, you have to talk to me about this

sooner or later," Kate argued. "And if not me, then your mom and dad."

Chelsea stopped dead in her tracks. An elderly couple walking arm in arm nearly plowed into her. "Don't you dare tell my parents," Chelsea warned.

Kate felt her jaw drop. "You're not telling them?"

"I'm not sure," Chelsea confessed. "I haven't decided what to do about that." Suddenly the strength seemed to drain out of her. She bit her bottom lip, dropping her eyes to avoid Kate's stare.

"Come on, Chelsea," Kate said. "Let's talk." She stepped closer and pulled Chelsea toward the sand. It still carried a trace of its daytime heat. They walked in silence down toward the water's edge. The tide was low, and the waves were gentle. Kate sat cross-legged on the cooling sand, and after a moment Chelsea joined her.

"Chels," she said softly. "We've always been there for each other. I count on your advice, and you count on mine." Kate reached for a broken shell and hurled it out to sea. "Remember when I was in eighth grade and I wanted to dye my hair red?"

Chelsea nodded sullenly. "You thought your boobs were too small," she recalled. "And that having red hair would make you look sexier."

"And you told me I'd end up looking like

Little Orphan Annie, and besides, my boobs would grow."

"I got the first part right, anyway."

"The point is," Kate said, grinning, "I listened to you, and you kept me from making a really idiotic mistake."

Chelsea turned to Kate, her gaze hardened. "And that's what Connor is? A really idiotic mistake?"

"That's what *marrying* Connor would be."

Chelsea looked away, and Kate realized how harsh she'd sounded. "Chelsea, I think I understand how you feel," she said. "I love Justin with all my heart. I'm really scared about what will happen to us when the summer ends. But that doesn't mean I'd even consider getting married at this point in my life."

"I'm not you, Kate." Chelsea lay back on the sand and closed her eyes. "And Connor's not Justin."

"But what about college? What about your art?"

"Who said I'm not going to college?"

"So what's the plan? You and Connor and I room together?"

Chelsea opened her eyes and rolled onto her side. "I'm sorry about that part, Kate," she said, her voice gentler. "But you can get another roommate. Someone who's not such a big slob. Or maybe," she added hopefully, "we could all rent an apartment together near campus."

Kate felt her throat tighten. She reached for a handful of sand and let it rain through her fingers. It was incredible. In the space of a few minutes Chelsea had gone from best friend to complete stranger.

"Look, Chelsea," Kate said in a strained voice, "I promise I'll try to understand if you'll just tell me one thing."

"What?"

"Why now? Why do you and Connor have to get married *now?*"

Chelsea sat up, still avoiding Kate's gaze, her eyes on a gull swooping in to inspect a nearby sandwich crust. Long moments passed. "I know what you're thinking, Kate," she said at last. "I'm only eighteen. I've never even had a serious boyfriend except Greg, and he was a major jerk, which shows I have questionable taste in men. I'm a sheltered, naive virgin who's about to make the worst mistake of her life." Her lower lip began to tremble. "And you're thinking I'm a lousy excuse for a best friend."

She was hiding something, something big. But whatever it was, she didn't trust Kate enough to tell her.

"You got that last part wrong," Kate said, feeling utterly defeated. "I'm thinking that *I'm* the lousy best friend."

eight

Grace walked along the main drag that sliced O.C. in half. When she'd left the house, she'd seen Kate and Chelsea walking toward the boardwalk, so naturally Grace had headed in another direction. It wasn't as scenic, but then, scenery wasn't what she was after.

The sudden onslaught of the craving had stunned her. One minute she was fine, listening with amusement to the tense, weird chatter of her housemates, the next, she was seeing that beer in Connor's hand and seeing nothing else.

She could feel the smooth, wet bottle in the palm of her hand. She could smell the malty aroma as it rose to her mouth, taste the bitterness on her tongue. It was sickening. It was as if someone else had seized control of her brain. It couldn't be her own mind that had wanted to leap like a lioness going for the throat of a gazelle. She wasn't like that. *She* was cool. She was in control. She wasn't screaming inside with need, shaking with the effort to restrain herself.

Not Grace Caywood.

A car slowed as it passed, horn blaring. A shout was snatched away by the wind. Grace looked down and realized that she had stepped off the curb into the street.

Across the busy six lanes was a bar, one of dozens in Ocean City. She didn't have her fake ID with her, though. And they would definitely card her, an upscale place like that. Ahead was a 7-Eleven. Same story. They would be sure to card her. If she was going to get a drink, it would have to be farther downtown, in the seedier section, where the street drunks sat in alleyways drinking from crumpled paper bags.

The image shocked her back to awareness. How effortlessly she had slipped over the line. She wasn't just thinking about a drink anymore. She was planning how to get one.

But she'd decided not to drink. She'd decided that. She'd told David she wouldn't. She'd told Bo.

Not that either of them would have to know.

Grace crossed the highway, drawn toward the dark, narrow streets that ran perpendicular to the boardwalk. She plunged into a block-long side street lined with ramshackle wood-frame buildings. Cheap rentals and cheaper businesses. There was a liquor store in the middle of the block, a place with a narrow, oil-stained parking lot and windows filled with yellowing posters of Jim Beam and Coors.

She'd been here before. There would be someone around in the alley next to the store, someone who could buy her what she needed.

"Racey Gracie," a loud voice boomed cheerfully.

Grace spun on her heels, feeling guilty and angry all at once. It was the girl who'd known David. Big Betty. Beth whatever her name was.

She was as sloppy as before, in her over-sized faded gray shorts. A ratty T-shirt with the logo of a local restaurant chain and torn, dirty white sneakers completed the ensemble. Her stringy blond hair framed a round face and shrewd, intelligent eyes.

Grace nodded at her. "Beth." She licked her lips and swallowed.

"Ah, this time you remembered." Beth pantomimed surprise. "I'm flattered."

"Yeah, well, nice seeing you again. I, uh, I . . ." Grace glanced toward the liquor store. "I have to meet someone."

"A guy, no doubt," Beth said.

Grace forced a smile. "That's right. You know me."

"Someone I know, perhaps? Johnnie Walker?

Jack Daniels? Bud Wiser?" Beth laughed heartily at her own joke. "I'm on particularly intimate terms with Bud. We're old pals."

Grace felt a surge of anger. "Is that what you think? You think I was going in there?"

"I know you were going in there," Beth said, still grinning.

"So what are you doing here?" Grace challenged. "Could it be *you're* going in?"

"No," Beth said, suddenly serious. "That couldn't be." Then she smiled again. "I live around here."

Grace made a point of dramatically curling her lip.

"Yes, reason enough to drink," Beth said.

"How about if you waddle back to your tacky home and leave me alone?" Grace snapped. She was tired of trying to be nice. It wasn't worth the effort. Neither was lying. She was going to get a drink, and she didn't give a damn if Beth knew it or what she thought about it.

But Beth just laughed. "You'll have to do a lot better than that, Racey Gracie. I was raised on insults."

"Maybe you had them coming," Grace said.

Beth looked at her with a direct gaze that made Grace squirm. "It was sudden, wasn't it? Shocked you. Scared you. One second you were okay, the next . . ."

Grace lowered her face. "Look, I'm sorry I was a bitch. But just leave me alone, okay?"

"I think we're sort of like vampires," Beth offered. "Ever read any vampire books? Anne Rice? Bram Stoker?"

Grace started to walk away, but something in Beth's voice held her. It had taken on a mystical, compelling quality. "Vampires," Beth continued, "torn apart by terrible, unnatural cravings that drive us to say and do things that even we find repellent. Driven by a need that others don't share and don't understand. Cursed."

"Wonderful metaphor," Grace said, trying to sneer and failing.

"It's a simile, actually. Alcoholics are *like* vampires. Simile."

"Go to hell."

Beth shrugged her beefy shoulders. "Let's go for a walk instead."

Suddenly Grace felt incredibly weary. "Walk?" she said quietly. "Where?"

"Nowhere," Beth said. "We just keep moving until the craving burns itself out."

Kate found Justin by following the sound of his hammer. He was inside his boat, lying flat on his back. An orange extension cord trailed behind him, a bulb burning brightly at the end.

"Justin," she called, crouching down to his level.

He stopped hammering for a moment and responded with a bright, enthusiastic hello. Then he went back to hammering. Between the blows Kate could hear him whistling—something he never did.

"Justin? Do you think you'll be done soon?"

This time the hammering didn't stop. "No. I'm feeling pretty charged up, and I want to get this berth seated just right."

Kate sat on the sawdust-covered floor and crossed her legs. "I think we should talk."

"Can't it wait?"

Kate rolled her eyes. "I'd rather not wait, no."

The hammering stopped, and Justin tilted his head up to see her. "What's this about?"

"What do you think it's about?" Kate asked, unable to control the sarcasm in her voice. "Your father appears out of nowhere and you refuse to talk to him. Then, a few minutes later, I find out my best friend is planning to get married. What's there to talk about?"

Justin raised his hammer again, then seemed to reconsider and set it down. He shimmied out onto the deck of the boat.

"It's hot as hell in there. Want to go for a swim?"

Kate stared at him. "I thought we were going to talk."

"About my . . . about *him?*" Justin shook his

head firmly. "No. There's nothing to talk about." He stood up and pulled Kate to her feet.

"Okay," Kate said slowly. "We'll drop your father." *For now*, she added silently.

"Good, let's go in. I'm getting a little water in the bilges." He started to climb onto the dock. "I want to make sure it's not that hull patch. I need you to hold a flashlight."

"Justin, I'm not wearing a bathing suit," Kate argued.

"It's nighttime. Who's going to see anything?" He grinned. "Aside from me, that is."

Kate stripped quickly, dropping her clothes on the catwalk. Justin handed her a watertight flashlight, and the two of them slipped into the body-temperature water between the side of the boat and the dock. Kate snapped on the light and let herself submerge.

The beam lit the blue-and-white hull of the sailboat. She swept the flashlight across the wooden pilings crusted with seaweed and barnacles. Justin appeared in the beam, eerily white underwater. He was motioning her to follow him.

He dove down, rolled over to face upward, and, with a grin at her, slid beneath the keel of the boat. Kate followed, feeling her back scrape over the wet sand as she slid through the two-foot gap between the bottom of the boat and the bay floor.

On the other side she surfaced and sucked in fresh air before dropping down again. Justin pointed to a place on the hull where, in the slanted beam of the flashlight, she could see a square that wasn't quite as perfectly smooth as the rest of the hull. Justin ran his hands over it. Then he gave her a thumbs-up, and they both broke the surface.

"Patch is fine," Justin gasped, smoothing back his wet hair. He took the flashlight from her and set it on the catwalk. "Come on."

"Wait. I'm naked."

Justin grinned. A moment later he slapped his wet trunks on the catwalk. "Feel better now?"

He rolled over into a breaststroke and disappeared beyond the boathouse gate. Kate sighed and swam after him, out into the starlit water of the bay.

She'd expected a nice, leisurely swim, but Justin took off briskly—not all out, but fast enough that she had to make an effort to keep up.

They swam side by side, separated by an arm's length. Kate felt the slow burn in her shoulders first, then in her knees and the front of her thighs. Still Justin was powering on, pulling ahead by a length, each stroke perfectly executed, economical and efficient. Kate settled into his wake, coasting on his momentum.

They were well beyond the cool, deep

channel at the middle of the bay when Kate yelled, "Stop, already!" in a gasping voice.

Justin swam a few more strokes, then stopped, treading water, a ghostly shape surrounded by black water.

"I hope you're planning to carry me back," Kate said. "I'm beat."

"Stand up and take a rest," Justin said with a grin. He stopped treading water and stood still, visible from midchest upward.

Kate reached her right foot down and felt sand. It was so surprising, she had to laugh.

"This way," Justin said, leading her up the gentle slope of the sandbar. The water sank to waist level, and before long they were standing on moist sand.

Kate lay on her back, staring up at the moonless, star-speckled sky. Justin lay beside her. It was an incredible feeling, surrounded by black water and black sky, two pale, fragile figures who seemed to be floating in space.

For a long time they lay silent. Then Kate's thoughts were unavoidably drawn back to Chelsea. Chelsea and Connor. The future Mr. and Mrs. Riordan.

"Why?" Kate wondered aloud.

"What?"

"I was wondering about Chelsea," Kate explained.

"Oh." Justin sighed. "They'll probably get over it."

"I'm not so sure."

"People do get married at our age," Justin remarked. "Maybe she's pregnant."

"She's still a virgin," Kate said. Then she winced. "I probably shouldn't have told you that."

Justin rolled over and laid his hand on her stomach, propping his head up on his other hand. He gave her a smoldering look. "You were, too, until very recently."

"You weren't," Kate pointed out. "And unless you somehow concealed a condom on you, we are not going to do what you're thinking about."

Justin laughed quietly. "You think you can read my mind, don't you?"

"Was I wrong?"

"No. But it was a lucky guess." He lay back down.

"I mean," Kate continued, "she barely knows Connor."

"Sometimes true love strikes suddenly," Justin offered philosophically. "Also, Chelsea's kind of religious. Maybe she figures she can't have sex till she's married, and she wants to, and Connor wants to. . . ."

"You're saying she'd get married just so she

could have sex?" Kate shook her head. "What a guy thing to think. Connor might do that, maybe, but not Chelsea. No, there's something else going on in her head. I can always tell when she's keeping something from me." She thought for a moment. "It's got to be something about Connor. I've never totally trusted him."

"Tell me about it," Justin agreed. "All that bull about how he'd never played poker before, and then he takes me for thirteen bucks. He hustled all of us. Still, I like the guy."

"So does Chelsea," Kate said darkly. She glanced over at Justin. "All at once the two people I care most about are behaving pretty weirdly."

"Come on," Justin said, rising to his feet. "We don't want to rest too much or we'll be too stiff to get back in."

Kate stood reluctantly. She watched Justin wade into deeper water, enjoying the sight of his hard, muscular body, the confident way he moved. He was the guy of any girl's dream—smart, funny, tender, sexy. . . . But there was a big part of Justin still marked Off-limits. And she wondered if that sign would ever come down.

nine

Kate pulled her red convertible in behind Alec's Jeep. The fact that Alec's car was there didn't necessarily mean he was home since he and Justin walked to work. As Kate had hoped, Grace's royal blue Eclipse was gone. This morning she'd mentioned she had another flying lesson with David.

Kate hopped out and trotted across the lawn to the house. She had only forty minutes left of her lunch hour before she was due back at the Safe Seas Institute. Not that Shelby watched the clock, but Kate didn't want to abuse her boss's generosity.

She opened the door and stepped in the living room. "Anybody home?" she shouted.

The only sound came from the kitchen, where one of the refrigerators had developed an annoying rattle.

"Anyone home? Chelsea? Connor? Anyone?"

Kate tossed her purse on the couch, trying

to ignore the twinge of guilt that had nagged at her all the way here. She crept up the stairs on tiptoes until she realized how stupid she must look. "Kate, I can't believe you're going to do this," she muttered under her breath. But someday Chelsea would thank her. That is, if they were still talking.

"Anyone home?" she yelled again when she got to the top of the stairs. She opened the door to Chelsea's room and stepped inside, once more walking on tiptoes. Oh, well, if she was going to act like a criminal . . .

Chelsea's room was a mess, as usual. The bed unmade. The closet door wide open, revealing a tangled knot of clothes on the floor. More clothing strewn over a straight-backed chair. A damp-looking towel on the dresser.

The walls were covered with thumbtacked pictures, sketches in charcoal or pencil. Some more-elaborate works in pastels. There were photographs, too, some unsold shots she had taken on the job. There was a photo of Kate, showing her in a bathing suit she'd bought recently, the one she'd been afraid was too revealing. Kate peered closely. Definitely too revealing.

Kate turned her attention to Chelsea's drawings. Several pastels were of the view outside her window—the boathouse, the pier, the bay.

Three charcoal drawings showed Grace in the morning, staring glumly at a cup of coffee, her hair tousled while she somehow managed to look perfect just the same. There were sketches of Alec and Justin, including a rather nice one of Justin's well-defined shoulders and arms.

But mostly there were sketches of Connor. Connor's face, mouth curved in a wry smile, eyes questioning. She'd done a good job of capturing him. Chelsea romanticized him a little, maybe, making the eyes larger than they seemed to Kate, the shoulders broader.

She gazed around the room, suddenly feeling ridiculous and a little dirty. How could she ever explain this intrusion to Chelsea?

Kate went to the dresser and reluctantly opened a drawer. Panties and bras. "There's a clue, Sherlock," she said.

Socks and T-shirts filled the next drawer. The third drawer held more T-shirts, a few thin sweaters, and an unopened pair of panty hose. The bottom drawer contained sweaters. Kate slipped her hand under the sweaters and touched a lump. She carefully lifted out the sweater. A black book with gilt edges and the name *Chelsea Lennox* inscribed in gold-leaf calligraphy on the cover. A Bible.

"Wonderful. Now I really feel good." Kate groaned.

She closed the drawer and stood. This was stupid. If there was something fishy going on, it involved Connor, not Chelsea.

Connor's room felt alien and a little threatening. It had the same undefinably male feel as Justin's boathouse loft. It was just as spare, if a little neater. Connor's bed was made, a chore Justin never bothered with. His dirty clothing was in a plastic basket. There was a tiny, narrow wooden desk placed directly in front of the single window. The top of the desk was empty. By the bed sat a rickety bookshelf, mostly filled with paperbound copies of poetry books. Dylan Thomas. Seamus Heany. W. B. Yeats.

"Almost *too* neat," Kate said aloud. "And thank you for that brilliant insight, Nancy Drew."

Grimly determined to carry on, Kate opened the desk drawer. It held a bundle of letters, a cloth-bound journal, a copy of a Tom Clancy novel, and a pair of yellow notepads.

Kate sat down in the chair, picked up the journal, and opened it. It was written in pencil, page after page of poems, essays, epigrams.

"Any good?"

Kate yelped, the journal went flying, and she shot to her feet, slamming her leg against the desk drawer.

Grace leaned against the doorjamb, looking like she could barely contain her delight.

"Damn it, Grace, you scared me to death," Kate yelled.

"I should have knocked," Grace admitted, a mocking glint in her eyes. "But then, it was obvious that you hadn't."

Kate sank back into the chair. There wasn't much point in trying to bluff her way out. Grace had caught her red-handed. She shrugged and picked the journal up off the floor. "It's this wedding thing."

"Oh yeah," Grace said, as if she'd forgotten. "The wedding thing."

"Chelsea won't listen to me," Kate said, "and she won't explain why she's doing it."

"So you break into her boyfriend's room, looking for answers." Grace laughed. "You're going to make someone a great mother some-day, Kate. Either that or you can get a job with the government. Kate Quinn, secret agent."

Kate blushed and felt her face grow hot. "I didn't know what else to do. It was stupid, and now I feel like a jerk. No, that's not true—I felt like a jerk from the start."

"So, you find anything?" Grace came in and began perusing Connor's books.

"His poetry's not bad," Kate offered lamely.

"He has good taste," Grace said. "Any English

teacher would approve of this collection. Did you find any hidden *Playboys*?"

"He doesn't seem to go in for anything worse than Tom Clancy," Kate said.

Grace bent over Connor's bed and slid her hand between the mattress and the box springs. She felt around for a moment and pulled out a magazine.

"How did you know?" Kate asked.

"Guys." Grace cocked her eyebrows in an expression of worldly wisdom. "They're very predictable, really."

"It's women who are hard to understand," Kate said, watching Grace return the magazine to its hiding place. "I've known Chelsea forever, and I don't have a clue why she's doing this."

Grace snorted. "Kate, Kate, Kate. Despite your little foray into burglary here, you're just too pure and innocent for your own good."

Kate stared at her, mystified.

"Are you really this naive?" Grace asked. "Can't you figure it out? There's a big difference between Chelsea and Connor, and I don't mean that she's black and he's white."

"What are you talking about, then?" Kate demanded.

"She's an American citizen. He's not. It's elementary, my dear Watson. The answer isn't in what you found, it's in what you didn't find—a green card."

"A what?"

"A green card. To let Connor stay in the United States legally. He's an Irish illegal. Ocean City's full of them, always has been."

Kate felt the blood drain out of her face. Of course. She *was* naive. "And if he marries an American . . ."

"He gets a green card, of course." Grace laughed again. "I figured you knew. I thought it was obvious."

Alec stepped into the antiseptic coolness of the clinic and shivered. It was a shock after the steamy ninety-three-degree heat he'd been simmering in all morning. He waved at the clinic receptionist. "I'm just going back to see Marta."

"Wait," the receptionist called out from behind her sliding glass window. "She's not in."

Alec stopped and backpedaled to peer through the glass. "Marta's not in?"

"She's at lunch."

"At lunch?"

"Yes."

Alec stared at the woman doubtfully. "It's only a few minutes after noon."

"She left with a couple of guys about ten minutes ago."

Alec felt his jaw clench. "Guys? A *couple*?"

"I don't think it's what you think," the receptionist said with a hint of a smile.

"Of course it isn't," Alec snapped. "Did they say where they were going?"

The receptionist shrugged and picked up a ringing phone.

Marta gone to lunch with not one but two guys? Well, the receptionist said they'd just left. How far could a girl in a wheelchair get in that amount of time? Even with *two* guys to help push it.

He turned on his heel and strode quickly back onto the boardwalk. Ten minutes. In ten minutes she could only reach . . . he looked both ways . . . about twenty different restaurants. Twenty? That could take a while. He squared his shoulders.

The first three restaurants hadn't seated a woman in a wheelchair. The fourth restaurant had, but she was ninety years old. Twenty minutes passed before Alec finally found Marta in a small gourmet restaurant half a block off the boardwalk.

She was at a round table in the center of the room, with her back to him. Sharing the table were two men. The first wasn't anything to worry about, a middle-aged guy with thinning dark hair. The other guy was a different story. He was younger, maybe midtwenties, tall, with a mane of wavy brown hair and perfect teeth.

As Alec watched, Marta reached across the table and touched the right hand of the younger man.

"Damn!" Alec muttered.

The hostess looked at him and raised an eyebrow. "May I help you?"

"No," Alec said automatically. Then he changed his mind. "Yes. See that girl over there? The one in the wheelchair?"

The hostess followed the direction he was pointing. "Yes."

"Would you tell her that Alec would like to speak to her?"

"You're welcome to go in and speak to her yourself."

"No. Just tell her, all right? I'll wait here."

The hostess sighed wearily but complied. Marta turned to look over her shoulder at Alec, her expression running from surprise to annoyance. And guilt? Had there been at least a little guilt?

Marta said something to her lunch companions and pushed away from the table. She followed the hostess, fixing Alec with a challenging stare.

"Alec. What are you doing here?"

"I was looking for you," Alec said.

"Why?"

"I wanted to have lunch with you—why do you think?"

Marta took a deep breath and maneuvered her chair out of the way of a group of diners coming in the door. "You should've let me know in advance."

"In advance?" Alec echoed loudly. "I have to tell you in advance when I want to see you?"

"Yes," Marta said, nodding.

"Why, because otherwise you'll go out with other guys?" Alec waved his arm toward the two men. "I thought Justin was just kidding when he said that. Now it looks like maybe he knew something."

Marta's eyes narrowed. "I have no idea what you're talking about. What has Justin got to do with anything?"

"Nothing," Alec said. "Never mind. That's not the point. That guy with the teeth is the point."

"Look, Alec, I don't remember us ever deciding that I was your sole property."

"Well, I didn't think you'd be going out with other guys," Alec said, suppressing the urge to yell. "I assumed that . . . that you'd only have me to go out with. I mean, I didn't expect . . ." What did he mean? He hadn't really thought it through all the way. And now he had the sense he'd stuck his foot way, way into his mouth.

Marta was quick with her own conclusion. "You mean you didn't think it was even possible I might have other guys interested, right?" Marta asked, her voice acid. "What with me being in a wheelchair."

"That's not it," Alec argued frantically.

"That's exactly it," Marta snapped. "I'm crippled and you're Joe Stud, so there's no way you should ever have to worry about competition. After all, you're doing me a big favor going out with me."

"That's not true," Alec said. "How would you feel if I went out with other girls?"

"I don't know," Marta said.

"Well, is that what you want? You want us *both* to be able to go out with other people? I mean, hey, it's not like I have trouble meeting girls."

"I'm sure you don't," Marta said. "While I, a girl with wheels instead of legs, am so lucky that the mighty Alec Daniels even deigned to look at me, let alone kiss me."

"You could do worse."

"So could you," Marta replied. "And I won't be in a relationship where you think going out with me is some kind of noble act of pity."

"I don't think that," Alec protested.

Marta stared at him shrewdly. "No, not entirely, but enough that it will be a problem until you get over it."

"Are you telling me you want to see other guys?"

"I'm telling you I want to see you, Alec," Marta said, "but I also want the right to see other guys if I choose to."

"Then the same thing would apply to me?"

"Absolutely."

"Fine." Alec turned to storm away and then hesitated. "So are we still on for tonight?"

"Sure, Alec," Marta said serenely.

"Fine," Alec snapped again. He threw open the door and stepped out onto the boardwalk. If that's the way she wanted it, great. It wasn't like he had trouble meeting girls. And it wasn't like he had a hard time getting them to say yes, either.

His angry gaze settled on a redhead who was practically spilling out of her string-bikini top. "Hi," he said brusquely. "My name's Alec. I'm a lifeguard. You want to go out with me?"

The girl froze, staring at him as if he were crazy.

Behind her a very large man loomed. "Hi.

My name's Jack. I'm her husband. You want to run that by us again?"

"Sorry," Alec muttered.

Well, that didn't prove a thing. Ocean City was still full of babes. And he wasn't going to eat himself up over Marta.

ten

Chelsea trudged up the porch steps on tired, hot, swollen feet. Walking the beach from ten to five every day wasn't easy work, especially when you were lugging a still camera, a video camera, and tons of accessories. She opened the door and welcomed the cool breeze from the ceiling fan. The living room smelled of buttered popcorn.

"Chelsea! You're home," Kate cried, leaping up from the couch she'd been sharing with Grace. She held a thick magazine in her hand. Grace held another, and there were more spread out on the coffee table.

"Uh-huh," Chelsea acknowledged, narrowing her eyes at Kate. "Aren't you home a little early?"

"Actually, I've been home all afternoon," Kate said. "I felt a little queasy after lunch, so I asked Shelby if I could bail, and she cut me loose. I feel fine now, though, and Grace and I have been having a great time planning."

Grace and I? Kate and Grace weren't exactly the best of friends. "Planning what?"

Kate laughed loudly. "Your wedding, of course."

Chelsea plopped down on the vacant couch, stretching out her legs and kicking off her shoes. "Kate, last I heard you thought I was insane to get married at all. Remember? College? Great big world out there? Why rush? Why trap yourself? All that?"

Kate shrugged. "Look, I still believe it," she admitted. "But if you're determined to do this, then, well, I *am* still your best friend, aren't I?"

Chelsea frowned. Was that actually a quaver in Kate's voice? "Look, I don't think it's going to be a big deal. I mean, we figured we'd do it down at city hall. Twenty bucks for the license and the judge, a ten-minute ceremony, and we're all done."

"How romantic," Grace cooed.

Kate shook her head. "A ten-minute ceremony? At city hall? No way. This is the biggest day of your life."

"It is?"

"Chelsea, stop kidding around," Kate chided. "You get married forever. Till death do you part."

"Or till you can't stand each other, whichever comes first," Grace added.

Kate shot her a quick glare. "Correct me if I'm wrong, but in the Roman Catholic Church, marriage is a sacrament, and it can't be undone."

"No divorce?" Grace asked, horrified.

"Nope." Kate turned back to Chelsea. "I am right about that, aren't I?"

Chelsea nodded. Yes, that was right. If you were married in the church, you were married, period. True, she'd been planning to do just the civil ceremony. But did that mean she wouldn't be married in the eyes of the church? How did all this work, anyway?

Her eyes rested on the magazines Kate and Grace had spread out on the table. *Brides. Modern Bride. Bridal Trends.* Each cover featured a radiantly happy face surrounded by mountains of white lace.

Grace thumbed through a copy of *The Bridal Guide* and held up a picture for Chelsea to look at. "What do you think of this?"

"What is it?"

"A bridesmaid's dress," Grace said. "I'm just thinking if it were me—I mean, if I were one of the bridesmaids—I wouldn't mind this because it's in a color you could actually wear again."

Kate winced. "I don't think Chelsea's really

gotten around to thinking about who her bridesmaids are going to be, Grace."

"Oh," Grace said. "I wasn't implying I should be one. I mean, Chelsea hasn't known me all that long, and you know, I'd understand if she had other people in mind."

"I don't have anyone in mind yet," Chelsea protested. There were some friends back home who would probably want to be included, but how could she get them to come without her parents finding out? "Wait a minute!" Chelsea said. What was she thinking? "I'm not having bridesmaids because we're just going to city hall."

"No bridesmaids? Not even me?" Kate said in a hurt voice.

"Do I have to think about this now?" Chelsea whined. "I just got home from work. My feet are killing me. I just want to take a shower and watch TV."

"Oh, you're right," Kate said. "Sorry. We were just kind of getting into it."

Chelsea stood and stretched. She felt a killer headache coming on. "Don't get all excited about this, all right?" she said irritably, heading for the stairs. "It's really no big deal."

"Whatever you say, Chels," Kate called after her. "But while you're taking a shower, think about what kind of flowers you like."

*　　*　　*

It hadn't been hard at all. She'd been lying right in front of Alec's chair all afternoon, wearing a skimpy bikini and slathering her tan, fit body with oil every few minutes.

She wasn't the first girl to do so. She was just the first to do so after his argument with Marta.

"Hi," she'd said.

"Hi, back," he'd answered.

"My name's Talon."

Sure, it is, he'd thought.

Now Talon was beside him in his Jeep as they drove down the main drag, past little restaurants and littler shops and the Putt-Putt golf course that featured twelve-foot fiberglass dinosaurs. She had slipped on a pair of shorts before leaving the beach. They hid a little more than the bathing suit had, but not much.

Her blond hair was a tornado swirling around her face. It reminded him of the way Marta's dark wavy hair whipped in the wind as they drove.

"So. Did you want to get something to eat?" Alec asked, raising his voice to be heard over the wind.

Talon turned in her seat, lifting one perfectly tanned knee to press ever so casually against his thigh. "What do *you* want to do?" she asked coyly.

"Are you hungry?"

Talon shrugged. "I could be if you are. Or I could not be if you just want to go to my place."

That did not remind him of Marta, Alec realized with grim satisfaction. He couldn't remember a single exchange they'd ever had when Marta did not have very definite ideas about what they should do and where they should go.

"Let's go to a drive through, pick something up," Alec said. "You want burgers or chicken?"

"Whatever."

"Pizza?"

"I eat whatever."

Flexible. That was nice for a change. "You like tacos?" Alec asked.

"I don't really care. Food is food, I guess."

Okay. "Maybe we should go straight to your place," Alec said. "After all, that is what I said I'd do. Drive you home."

"Uh-huh." She looked at him, eyes trailing the length of his body. "You are so cut."

"Thanks." Alec felt his face heat up. "So are you."

"What do you do?"

He looked over at her in confusion. "I'm a lifeguard."

"Duh. I meant, what do you do to stay in shape?"

"Oh." Alec laughed uncomfortably. "I mostly just swim, run a little. I lifted weights for a while, but I've kind of gotten out of the habit."

"Do you do steroids?"

"No way," Alec said forcefully.

"Do you, like, run a certain number of miles every day?" Talon asked.

Is this drive taking forever? Alec wondered. Traffic seemed to be moving well, but it felt like they'd been driving for half an hour. "I try to do five or six miles a day. But look, it's dull talking about me. How about if we talk about you?"

"Okay."

"Well, what do you want to be?" *Great, Alec, dork question of the century.* "I mean, are you going to college?"

Talon laughed. "I don't think so."

I don't think you are, either, Alec thought. "So, no college. That's cool. What are you going to do?"

"You mean, like at the end of summer?" Talon asked, brows knitted. "Because right now I have a job."

"Really? What do you do?" Alec asked, trying to sound interested.

"I'm a dancer."

"Like a ballerina?"

"Puh-leeze." She did a little shimmy. "An *exotic* dancer."

Why was he not surprised? "So," Alec said wearily.

Alec pressed down harder on the accelerator.

"Where are you going? We passed my street."

"You didn't tell me," Alec said, his voice edged with annoyance.

"It's Seventy-eighth Street," Talon said.

Alec pulled the Jeep into a right turn, then turned right again and raced back south toward Seventy-eighth Street. Talon pointed to her building, and he pulled to a stop in front of it.

"Come on," she said with a giggle as she hopped out.

Alec glanced at his watch. He was supposed to have met Marta at the house ten minutes ago. Not that it would kill her to wait. After all, she was the big freedom lover.

"I don't know," Alec said.

Talon came around to the driver's side and leaned in the window. "Don't you want to . . . you know?"

"You know?" Alec nearly swallowed his tongue.

"You are so cut," Talon said again. She put a hand on his biceps.

"Uh, yeah, thanks. And you're . . . you're really something."

"Is that good?"

Alec sighed. "It's great. Great hair. Great

face. Great legs. Great everything." *Great big empty space between your ears*, he added silently.

Talon smiled happily. "So come on."

Alec bit his lip. He glanced at his watch again. No guy worthy of being called a guy would walk away from this. And for what? For some bossy, hardheaded, opinionated girl?

He'd have to be an idiot.

"Chels, come on down. You have to read this," Kate called to Chelsea, who was standing on the stairs. "It's an article on how to write your own wedding vows."

Chelsea sighed. Marta had joined the group while she'd been upstairs showering, along with some girl she didn't know who was reclining in the La-Z-Boy. The four of them were thumbing happily through bridal magazines.

"I was going to work on a painting," Chelsea lied, motioning vaguely in the direction of her room.

"Chelsea, you haven't met Beth," Grace said. There was a tinge of distaste in her voice.

Chelsea nodded. They had her there. She put on a happy face and descended the rest of the way.

"Chelsea, this is Beth," Grace said, managing a little smile.

"An old drinking buddy," Beth said. She

raised an eyebrow to show she was joking.

Grace's jaw tensed. "We knew each other in school."

"More like we knew *of* each other," Beth corrected matter-of-factly. "I was required to bow and tug my forelock whenever Grace passed by."

Kate and Marta burst out laughing, while Grace narrowed her almond eyes and tightened her lips.

"Now we're buddies," Beth went on. "It's an A.A. thing. A more stable drunk hooks up with an unstable drunk to help her stay on the straight and narrow."

"Yes, and aren't I lucky Beth seems to have chosen me?" Grace said.

"I like to think of it as fate," Beth said.

"Anyway," Kate said, "anyway, we thought we'd all go down to the mall with you, Chels."

"What for?" Chelsea asked.

"To look at wedding dresses. And you know—your trousseau."

Chelsea sent Kate a suspicious look. "Kate, first of all, you're against me getting married, and second of all, I can't believe the word *trousseau* just came out of your feminist mouth."

"Hell, we all think you're stupid to get married," Grace said. "But we all like to shop."

"Especially for wedding-related stuff,"

Marta agreed. "It's a whole new challenge."

"I don't think you're stupid," Beth said. "I don't even know you. I'd have to know much more about the circumstances before I could think you're stupid."

"She's eighteen, she's never even done the dirty deed, and she's marrying a guy she's known less than a month," Grace told Beth. "That's all you need to know."

"I was supposed to be meeting Alec here," Marta said thoughtfully. "But he hasn't shown yet, so I guess I can go with you guys. We can take my van."

"Where is Alec?" Chelsea wondered. "I'm sure he'll be here soon. Maybe you should wait."

Marta waved off the suggestion. "It's deliberate. He's trying to teach me a lesson or something. If I'm gone by the time he finally wanders in, he'll be mad." Marta chuckled. "Teach *me* a lesson. I'll teach *him* a lesson."

"That's it, Marta," Grace said with a wink, "show him who's boss."

"Don't you have to tell Justin you're going out?" Chelsea asked Kate, making one last-ditch effort to avoid a no doubt annoying and embarrassing trip.

"Tell Justin?" Kate looked surprised. "That's the kind of thing married people do, Chelsea."

eleven

"What size do you think Connor is?" Kate asked Chelsea.

"Ex*cuse* me?"

"What size suit?" Kate said, rolling her eyes. She pointed toward the formal-wear store across the food court. "If we knew his size, we could reserve a tux for him."

"A tuxedo? Connor's not going to wear a tuxedo," Chelsea said, laughing. "I'll be lucky if he doesn't show up in that ratty bathrobe of his."

"Of course he'll wear a tux," Grace said. "It would give him some class."

"Even if I wanted him to," Chelsea argued, "I could never convince him."

Marta shook her head. "If it were me, I could convince him."

Kate noted the confused, uncertain expression on Chelsea's face. Perfect. It was beginning to work. Grace's plan was brilliant. The bigger deal they made out of the wedding, the more Chelsea would have to think about it, and the more she thought, the more (Kate hoped) she would doubt her decision.

"I am so sick of this mall," Grace said suddenly as they made their way past yet another swimsuit boutique.

"I like the mall, myself," Beth said. "Especially on a rainy day when all the tourists come streaming off the beaches and crowd in here. I revel in that desperate need they have to squeeze some enjoyment out of their vacation. Deprived of the beaches, they have to convince themselves that yes, cruising this mall, dragging their kids from store to store exactly like they do every Saturday back home, is a good time."

"You have a perverse sense of fun," Grace muttered.

"That's what it takes to enjoy Ocean City as a local," Beth said. "A perverse sense of fun."

"I've seen this mall," Grace said flatly. "I've seen every store, every shelf, every item on every shelf. I've eaten all the food in the food court. I've probably parked in every parking space. It's like the rest of this town: old news."

"Are you always this much fun, Grace?" Marta asked.

"Now, in New York or Chicago or Los Angeles, you have malls, plural," Grace said. "Tired of one, they build another."

"No," Marta disagreed. "You're wrong. All malls are the same."

"Aha." Kate pointed. "Trousseau city."

" 'Secret Moments'?" Chelsea made a face.

Kate grabbed her by the arm and pulled her along. The rest of the girls followed them into the store. The walls and carpet were pastel pink, and the air was thick with perfume.

"Wow. Who wears this stuff?" Chelsea wondered, gazing at an elaborately frilled black teddy.

Grace picked up a tiny bit of white lace and held it up next to Chelsea. "Here. How about this?"

"Get rid of that thing." Chelsea pushed the garment away. "Someone might see me."

"I kind of like it," Marta said thoughtfully.

"Me too," Beth agreed.

"I'll bet Connor would like it," Grace said, wiggling her eyebrows suggestively.

"He'd laugh himself sick if I wore that."

"No, he wouldn't," Grace said. "Guys love this stuff. She paused for a beat, then let a slow half smile form. "Trust me."

Kate shot her a glance. Was that Justin she'd been thinking about? No, not Justin. Well, maybe Justin. She held the teddy up to herself.

"Is there anything I can help you ladies with?" A salesgirl appeared.

"Yes," Beth said quickly. "We'd like something

sexy that all five of us would look equally good in."

The salesgirl swallowed, her eyes filling with panic, while Grace and Marta both burst out laughing.

"Actually, our friend here is getting married," Kate said smoothly, pushing Chelsea forward. "She needs something appropriate for, you know, her big wedding night."

"Honeymoon attire," Grace said.

"Something that says, 'I'm yours, you big strong man, all yours,'" Marta elaborated.

"Congratulations," the salesgirl said to Chelsea. "We get a lot of women customers coming in to buy for such an occasion. Were you thinking of something along the lines of a teddy? Or perhaps a nice negligee? We have a lovely set in red lace that's on sale."

Chelsea rubbed her eyes. "I just wanted to go to city hall. Ten-minute ceremony. No big deal."

"She's shy," Kate explained.

"Excuse me," Chelsea said, "but I'm very thirsty. I'm going to buy myself a Coke."

"That's all right," Kate said soothingly as Chelsea started to leave. "We'll all pitch in and get you something nice. A wedding present."

"Don't you dare," Chelsea grumbled.

"If we're not here, we'll be down at the bridal shop," Kate called, but Chelsea was already gone.

Grace stuck out her palm, and Kate slapped it. "Grace, you're a devious person," Kate said. "I think it's starting to work."

"What are you two talking about?" Marta asked suspiciously.

"Chelsea's my best friend in the world," Kate said. "I'm not going to let her screw up her life by getting married straight out of high school."

Marta frowned. "But . . . but you've been acting like you were excited."

"Grace's idea—use reverse psychology."

"Chelsea wants to get married," Grace explained, "and if we fight her, she'll only dig in her heels. That's the theory, anyway. We'll make a big deal out of it—bachelorette party, arrange to schedule the ceremony as soon as possible at her church, *not* at city hall, do the whole rehearsal thing."

"In other words, if she wants a wedding, we're going to give her one," Kate said with determination. "With a vengeance."

Alec checked his watch again as he pulled the car to a stop. He hopped out and ran toward the house. Then he stopped himself. No, he was not going to run inside. Marta would think he was rushing because he was late.

He was, but he didn't want her thinking that.

He opened the front door. The lingering smell of popcorn met his nose. Connor was lying back in the La-Z-Boy on full recline. He pried open one eye, then closed it again.

Justin wandered in from the direction of the kitchen. He was holding a piece of paper. "What exactly is a trousseau?" he asked.

"A what?" Alec asked distractedly. He wondered if Marta was upstairs with Chelsea or Kate. But that seemed unlikely. Marta couldn't exactly negotiate stairs with ease.

"A trousseau." Justin held up the note. "I found this note from Kate. She says she and Grace and Chelsea and Marta and some person named Beth went shopping for Chelsea's trousseau."

"Excuse me?" Connor yelped, bringing the recliner upright. "Trousseau?" He pronounced the word with obvious distaste.

"Yeah. What is it?"

"It's the stuff, the clothing and other things, a woman puts together to take into her married life," Connor explained, shaking his head.

"Oh," Justin said.

"You mean they're all gone? Marta went with them?" Alec cried. Marta and he had a date. Sure, he was a little late, but that didn't give her the right to take off and leave him hanging.

"Looks like they're all off shopping," Justin said. "Just us guys here this evening."

"You don't think the girl's going off to buy herself a wedding gown, do you?" Connor asked, his face tight.

"I imagine," Justin said. "I mean, she's getting married, right? Wedding, wedding gown. They kind of go together."

"Did Kate say in the note when they'd be back?" Alec demanded.

"It was supposed to be a small, private matter," Connor moaned. "Not a major production."

"I thought you knew something about women, Connor," Justin said. "A *small* wedding? Give me a break."

"It's just a formality, is all," Connor argued. "A little ceremony between two people who love each other."

Alec flopped down onto the couch and gave Connor a sour glance. "If you don't mind my asking, why are you getting married, anyway? I mean, it seems to me women are quick enough to mess up your life without making it legally binding."

Connor shot Justin a knowing look. "Must be a little trouble with Marta, I'm guessing."

"Looks that way," Justin agreed.

"I'm just asking why you'd want to get married," Alec persisted.

Connor looked away. "Oh, one thing or another. It has been a popular idea for a few millennia, you know."

Justin sat on the couch across from Alec and propped his feet on the coffee table, shoving aside a bridal magazine. "Do you mind if I ask a rude question?"

"Ask it and I'll decide," Connor replied.

"Is this because Chelsea won't sleep with you?"

Connor flushed. "Who told you she wouldn't?"

"My girlfriend is your girlfriend's best friend."

Connor shifted uncomfortably. "Well, it's true Chelsea takes the very traditional approach on those matters."

"And that's why you're marrying her?" Alec asked, raising his eyebrows. "Because if that's all you're looking for, I know the girl for you."

Justin and Connor both stared at him, openmouthed. "No, not Marta, you sleaze-balls," Alec said. "This other girl."

"Oh, really?" Connor said.

Justin nodded. "Yep, trouble with Marta."

"I'm not having trouble with Marta," Alec lied. "It's just that, you know, she was getting too possessive."

Alec hated the know-it-all look that passed between Connor and Justin. "Marta, possessive?" Justin mused. "Funny, that isn't how I think of her at all."

"So she's giving you the brush-off, eh?" Connor said.

Alec felt his face growing warm. "No, she's, you

126

know, we decided, the two of us, that we could see other people if we wanted to. No biggie."

"Ah," Justin said. "Hence the mythical other girl."

"See? I'm in a no-win situation here," Alec complained. "If I go out with another girl, everyone will ask how I could be such a jerk to Marta. And if I don't, everyone will say, 'How could you let Marta get you so whipped?'"

"I wouldn't say either of those things," Justin said. "All I'd say is if you screw up and lose Marta, you're an idiot."

"An idiot," Connor agreed, nodding.

"Look, let's cut the bull, all right?" Alec said harshly. "The only reason you guys say that is because Marta's in a wheelchair. I mean, that's the truth here."

"You think we like her only because she's disabled?" Justin demanded. "Is that why *you* like her?"

"No," Alec said quickly. "Of course not. But I know what people think. They think, oh, it's so sweet that guy is going out with her. It must be a pity date. Or else they think the opposite. You know—he's going out with her because a *normal* girl is too much of a challenge for him."

"Who cares what everyone else thinks?" Justin said.

"Easy for you to say," Alec replied softly. "No

one looks at you and Kate and wonders whether there's something weird, something not quite normal about the two of you." He dropped his head into his hands. "It gets in the way sometimes. She thinks maybe I'm thinking I'm doing her a favor. Who knows? Maybe I did think that at first. All I know is, I picked up this girl this afternoon with this stunning, amazing body. Beautiful. Ready to go, without me so much as asking. And I couldn't do it. She was boring. She was dumb. She didn't give me a hard time."

"Well, I don't think Marta needs your pity," Justin said.

"Me neither," Connor agreed. "I've seen you two together. I think she's the one who should be taking pity on you, after that pathetic story."

"Oh, and you're Mr. Cool, Connor?" Justin teased. "You're the one who's getting married."

Connor's smile quickly faded. "That's me," he said quietly. "Mr. Cool." After a moment he brightened. "So, are you fellows going to throw me a bachelor party?"

Justin shrugged. "Any excuse for a party, right?"

"Excellent." Connor rubbed his hands together. "Alec, this girl you were talking about. Do you think she'd jump out of a cake?"

"Hi, honey, I'm home," Kate called out cheerily. Justin stood up inside his boat and pulled off a pair of plastic safety goggles. He grinned and climbed out to greet her with a hug and a nice, lingering kiss. His arms were hot, covered with a fine sheen of sweat and little bits of wood shavings.

"All done with your shopping, dear?" he asked, adopting her tone.

"We went to the mall and looked for wedding gowns," Kate said. She freed herself from Justin's embrace and kicked off her shoes. "It turns out wedding gowns cost more than I'll make in the next five years. What have you been up to?"

"Well, I had this somewhat depressing conversation with Connor and Alec on the subject of women. Then I came out here to do some work."

No mention of his father, Kate noted. As if the man had never reappeared. "What did Connor have to say about women?" she asked.

"Not much. Connor is a guy who sounds like he's telling you his whole life story, and when he's done, you realize he hasn't told you a thing. No wonder he can play poker. You think he's an open book, but he keeps his hand well hidden."

"Guys are very good at hiding their real emotions," Kate said pointedly, but Justin showed no sign he'd caught the sarcasm.

"Not Alec," he said. "You can read that poor boy a mile away."

"Marta? Great. That'll be the next wedding we have to try to stop."

"Try to stop?" Justin repeated. "I thought you were just out shopping with Chelsea."

Kate smiled. "Things aren't always what they seem."

"Uh-huh." Justin picked up his watch from a worktable and checked it. "You know, it's only a little after eight. If you're not too tired, we could take in a quick movie."

"Let me guess, that new sailing—"

A knock at the door interrupted her. "Maybe Chelsea's come to tell us she's recovered her sanity and the wedding's off," Kate suggested.

Justin walked to the door and opened it. A second later he closed it again. He turned back toward Kate with a grim expression on his face.

From outside there came a firm voice. "Justin, sooner or later you're going to have to talk to me."

"I have work to do," Justin said in a low voice, staring hard at Kate. "I'll be down in my boat."

"Justin—" Kate began.

The voice spoke again. "Justin, I'm only asking for one hour of your time. One hour, and I'll leave you alone."

Justin's fists were clenched by his sides. His lips were pressed into a thin, bloodless line.

"Justin," his father said again, "talk to me. Otherwise I won't be able to leave."

Something in Justin's eyes seemed to collapse. He drew a deep, shaky breath. "Let him in, Kate," he whispered. "Let the jerk in."

Kate licked her lips nervously. "I'll let him in and go on up to the house," she said.

"No," Justin said sharply. "I want you here."

Kate nodded. She put her hand on the doorknob and opened it. Justin's father was dressed in blue jeans and a pale yellow cotton shirt. His expression was solemn. He was smaller than Justin, thinner, less muscled, but his frame was just as broad shouldered. His face wasn't much like his son's, though. The eyes were deeper, almost sunken. Only the mouth was the same, with the same wide, thoughtful half smile.

"Justin," he said.

"You have ten minutes of my time," Justin said coldly. "Say what you have to say and get out."

twelve

Justin stared hard at the man before him. He wouldn't let himself look away, and he wasn't about to show any trace of emotion. If this man thought he could just apologize and all would be forgiven, he had a surprise in store. There would be no forgiving, not ever.

"You look good," his father said.

Justin didn't answer.

The man glanced uncertainly at Kate. "Are you . . . ?"

"My name is Kate Quinn, Mr. Garrett," Kate said, extending her hand.

He shook it, smiling nervously. "My name's Turner. Jonathan Turner. After I left—"

"After you ran out," Justin snapped.

"Justin and his mother—"

"Your wife," Justin corrected. "The wife you ran out on."

"My ex-wife decided to change her name and Justin's to Garrett," he explained. "Her maiden name." He sighed and looked down at the floor. "Is there somewhere we can sit down?"

"No." Justin wasn't going to let this turn into anything remotely comfortable. No chitchat about old times. No drinks would be served.

"All right," Jonathan said. He twisted his mouth into a bitter smile. "Tough, aren't you? Good. It's a good thing for a man to be a little tough. I never was."

Justin pointedly lifted his watch from the table and looked at it. "We're hoping to make a movie."

"What do you want from me?" his father asked, his face pale.

Justin shook his head. "Nothing. You're the one who wanted to talk to me, remember?"

"I thought I would try to explain," Jonathan said softly. "I figured you must wonder about . . . about why I left."

"Ran out."

"All right," his father said, voice rising, "ran out, if that's the way you want it. You're right, I ran out. I was selfish. I was weak. I ran out because I couldn't take it anymore."

Justin allowed himself a cold, contemptuous smile.

His father's anger was burned out. He looked at the boat, nodding. "Your boat?"

Justin chose not to answer.

"Doing well enough for yourself, eh?" the man said. "Going to college?"

Justin tried not to let the answer show in his eyes, but his father nodded, anyway. "So, no college plans. Just a boat. Nice-size boat, too. Not many places a competent sailor couldn't take her."

Justin glanced uncertainly at Kate. She had drifted a little distance away but was watching his father intently.

His father smiled wistfully. "I guess some things are passed from father to son regardless. I like to sail myself."

"Your ten minutes are about up," Justin said, but the conviction had gone out of his voice. A memory from long ago had resurfaced, almost against his will. A memory of his father and him setting a toy sailboat down in a calm pond. His father had made the boat from a single piece of hardwood.

"Yeah, I had a fine boat, once upon a time," his father said sadly.

His father was remembering, too. Remembering a time before, when they'd still been father and son. And now, here Justin was with his own boat, rebuilt with his own hands. Funny how he had never connected up the two things in his mind.

"Well, I better get this over with," his father

said in a voice heavy with regret. "Whether you admit it or not, Justin, you want to know why I left. You wouldn't be human if you didn't."

Justin no longer trusted himself to respond. Something in the iron wall of his resolve had weakened. He let silence be his answer.

"I don't flatter myself that you still have any real feeling for me," his father went on. "If the situation were reversed, I wouldn't, either. I imagine your mother had some tough times afterward. I say imagine, because I cut myself off from all contact with her and with you. That's the way she wanted it, and—"

"The way *she* wanted it?" Justin demanded.

"Your mother. She said it had to be a clean, total break. She didn't want me to see you or be around you. She didn't want any child support, any contact whatsoever. I figured she'd probably change her mind about that last part, but by then I was bitter."

"You're saying Mom threw you out?" Justin asked incredulously.

"No," his father admitted. "I wanted out, for reasons of my own. All I wanted was to—" His voice broke, and it took several seconds before he regained control. "All I wanted was to go on being your father, but you see, Justin, your mom didn't want me infecting you with my own sick ideas."

Justin frowned. "What are you talking about? What ideas?"

"I was in love, Justin, with someone else."

"It happens," Justin said.

"I was in love with another man," his father said quietly. "I was gay. I mean," he amended with a crooked smile, "I am gay."

Justin felt the world stop turning. Nothing moved. Nothing breathed. No sound was made. He stared at the man before him, who was smiling a pleading smile. The man who had taught him to work on boats. The man who had sneaked ice cream to him when his mom sent him up to bed without supper. The man . . .

The man who had walked out on him, and his mother, because he was gay. No man at all.

"You've had your say," Justin whispered. "Now leave."

"Justin, you have to—"

"Leave!" Justin roared. His hands worked at his sides; his eyes felt like they might explode. "Get the hell out of my house!" He took a step forward, fists clenched, muscles tight.

His father took a step back. Then he disappeared into the night.

"Justin," Kate pleaded.

"Don't," Justin warned.

Kate grabbed him by the shoulders, turning him to face her. "Justin, you can't do this."

"Watch me."

Kate released him. Her expression was a mixture of horror and disappointment—everything he felt, too. Only his was directed at his father—and hers seemed to be at him. "No, I don't think I will," she said. She marched to the door and slammed it behind her.

Justin stood alone, torn between explosive, pent-up energy and complete exhaustion. He turned back toward his boat, picking up a hammer as he went. He took a few steps, then let the hammer slip. It clattered on the floor. He sat down heavily on the catwalk, his legs hanging over the water.

Then he leaned over, put his head in his hands, and, unable to stop himself, cried softly, the bitter tears falling into the water below.

Her dress was snow white, and behind her a train spread across fifty square feet of marble floor. There were flowers in her hand—green flowers, for some reason. The church was huge, with dark wooden pews lining each side of the aisle. On the right-hand side Chelsea recognized family members—aunts, uncles, cousins. But there were also, to her surprise, a number of celebrities—Halle Berry, Denzel Washington, Jesse Jackson. All of Boyz II Men were sitting in a pew, crammed in beside Spike Lee. They were all black—and all dressed in traditional African garb.

On the left side of the aisle were people with pale skin and freckles and red hair. Chelsea didn't recognize most of them, although Ted Kennedy stood out. Shania Twain stood near the front, hands folded demurely before her. For some reason Michael Jackson was with her, although technically he should have been on the other side of the church. Nearly everyone was holding a brown-and-yellow bottle of Guinness, including Michael Jackson.

Suddenly Chelsea was standing before the altar. Kate, dressed all in black, stood by silently with Justin, who was, as usual, wearing nothing but his red lifeguard trunks.

Connor appeared, grinning, in a dark green tuxedo. He also had a bottle of Guinness, but it was tucked in his coat pocket. "Top o' the mornin' to ye," he said. His face seemed indistinct, with features that kept shifting and changing. This puzzled Chelsea, even worried her a little, but just then the priest appeared.

It was Nelson Mandela, looking fierce in a beaded headdress and carrying a leather shield that clashed with his conservative business suit. He spoke angrily in a language Chelsea didn't understand.

Oddly, Connor seemed to have no trouble.

"Sure an' it's true," he said. "She's always after me Lucky Charms."

Mandela and Connor turned to look at Chelsea, waiting for her response. For a moment she felt panicky. Then, without conscious thought, her mouth opened and she gave the proper response. "They're magically delicious," she replied.

"Ye may kiss the Blarney Stone, lassie," Mandela said.

Chelsea woke with a start, her hand fumbling blindly for the clock-radio alarm. She found it and slapped the snooze button.

She sat up, her heart pounding wildly. Slowly she brought it under control. The clock showed nine. She climbed out of bed and pulled on her robe.

Dreams. They meant nothing. They were just distorted reflections of the previous day's events. That's what she believed.

Still. Nelson Mandela?

She opened the door to Kate's room, heading for the bathroom they shared, and let out a low whistle. "Well, well," she murmured.

Kate's bed had obviously been slept in, for the first time in quite a while. Evidently Kate and Justin were having a spat.

Chelsea showered quickly and changed into her work clothes, a pair of shorts and a bathing-suit top. She was on her way back to her room when the upstairs telephone rang. She lifted the receiver and heard the hiss and crackle of a bad long-distance connection.

"Hello?" she said.

The voice on the other end was a distant whisper. "Yes, I'm calling for Connor Riordan. Have I the right number?" It was a girl's voice, with a heavy Irish accent.

"Yes, he lives here," Chelsea replied, "but he's at work."

"Is he now," the voice said.

"Can I tell him who called?"

"Yes, you can tell him Molly rang him up to say hello."

"Okay, I'll give him the message."

The line went dead. Chelsea felt a queasy feeling, a sense of something gone wrong. After a moment she decided it was nothing but the lingering hangover from her dream. After all, seeing Shania Twain and Michael Jackson together was enough to unsettle anyone.

In the kitchen she started a small pot of coffee. When she reached to get an English muffin out of the refrigerator, she saw the note. It was from Kate.

"'Chels,'" she read out loud. "'Good news. Spoke with Father Tom at your church. Can squeeze you in Saturday A.M. Rehearsal Friday P.M. Your bridesmaid, Kate.'"

Chelsea crumpled the note slowly. Saturday. This was Wednesday.

Seventy-two hours more as carefree, young, irresponsible Chelsea Lennox.

thirteen

The front desk of the Ocean City Grand was a thirty-foot-long sweep of pink marble and brass. This time of day, a little past noon, there were quite a few people checking out—loud families with children, old people in matching blue polyester, prosperous middle-aged men wearing too much flashy gold jewelry, teenagers dressed for display. It took Kate a few minutes to reach a uniformed clerk.

"I'm looking for Jonathan Turner's room," she said. "Can you help me?"

"Is he registered at this hotel?" the young woman in a crisp navy suit asked irritably.

"Yes, only I don't know the room number."

The clerk asked Kate to repeat the name and tapped into her computer keyboard. "He checked out about fifteen minutes ago."

Kate cursed under her breath. "Sorry," she apologized. "It's just that it's kind of important. I'm taking my lunch hour to find him."

"I'm taking my lunch hour to work," the clerk grumbled. "You don't happen to know anyone who wants a hard, low-paying job, do you? We're shorthanded."

"No, I'm sorry," Kate said, smiling sympathetically. "Ocean City blues, huh? At the start of the season everyone's looking for a job. By the middle of the season every employer needs help."

The clerk raised her eyebrows in agreement. "Look, you might ask the bell captain. He may know if your friend went to the airport or on to another hotel."

"Thanks, I'll do that." Kate marched over to the bell stand. "Excuse me," she said to a guy about her age with a light blond crew cut, "I'm looking for a man who just checked out. Jonathan Turner?"

"Age?"

"Middle-aged, maybe forty. Big build but kind of skinny."

"Baseball cap?"

Kate snapped her fingers. "Yes, he did have one on."

The bell captain nodded. "Oh yeah. The guy and his *boy*friend. I'm holding their bags in the checkroom. Guy said he had a stop to make before he split town. Hasn't been gone more than maybe five, ten minutes."

Kate nodded and tore out of the lobby

onto the boardwalk, nearly colliding with an elderly woman carrying a giant bucket of caramel corn. Mr. Turner was obviously going to make one last attempt to speak to Justin before he left for good. If she ran, there was a chance she might catch up with him. Maybe somehow she could get Justin to see reason.

She was almost to Justin's section of the beach when she spotted the baseball cap bobbing back and forth amid a sea of heads. Mr. Turner was walking with a younger man.

Kate glanced to her left. Yes, this was Justin's section. He would either be in his chair or on his way to Floaters, depending on when Luis sent him to lunch.

But Mr. Turner and his friend kept walking. Kate fell in step behind them, feeling a little uncomfortable. This was the second time in as many days that she had tried to play detective. Justin's father stepped off the boardwalk near the clinic. With the crowd thinning, Kate held back. To her surprise Mr. Turner and his companion went straight to the clinic door and disappeared inside.

Great. Now what? Kate asked herself. She glanced at her watch. She was due back at Safe Seas in twenty-eight minutes. Ten minutes to get back to her car, ten minutes to drive. She had eight minutes until she had to get going.

She was down to two minutes when the clinic door opened and Justin's father and his friend reappeared—with Marta.

The younger man leaned down to give Marta a hug. Justin's father did the same, more tentatively. As he started to release her, Marta held him an extra few seconds, as if she were trying to make it last.

Then the younger man climbed into a waiting taxi. Mr. Turner paused at the car's door and gazed off toward the boardwalk. Kate worried for an instant that he might see her spying, but she realized that his gaze was far away. Then he slid into the cab and closed the door behind him.

Marta watched the taxi pull away. When it was gone, she sat there in her wheelchair, tilting back to enjoy the sun's rays. Kate's shadow fell across her.

"Hi, Marta," Kate said.

"Kate? So, you escaped from fish world?"

Kate smiled. "It's a long story." She hesitated, unsure of how to bring up her question. Strictly speaking, it was none of her business. "Marta, do you know that man who just left?"

"Not really," Marta responded with a shrug. "He's a tourist from L.A. Came to get a refill on his medicine. I guess his supply got lost with a piece of luggage. We got to talking about L.A. As a matter of fact," Marta added, grinning, "they took me to lunch yesterday, which got Alec very jealous."

"Mr. Turner, right?" Kate asked.

Marta shot her a suspicious look. "How do you know that?"

Kate sighed. "He used to be . . . he *is* Justin's father."

Marta's eyes went wide with surprise. *"Madre de Dios,"* she muttered, crossing herself quickly. Then she blushed. "Sorry. A habit I picked up from my dad." She shook her head. "Justin's father. He told me he was here to look up an old friend."

"Justin wasn't exactly ready with open arms."

Marta's dark eyes grew sad. "That's too bad."

"Marta, what was he at the clinic for?"

"Some medicine," Marta said evasively.

"What medicine?"

Marta sighed. "Kate, you know I can't tell you that. People who come to the clinic have a right to privacy."

Kate nodded slowly. "He has AIDS, doesn't he?"

Marta just stared straight ahead and bit her lip.

"He's dying," Kate whispered.

"He's had some bad periods already," Marta admitted. "I guess he's visiting all the places and people he cared about. You know—one last good-bye."

When Luis finally cut him loose for lunch, Justin decided he wasn't in the mood for yet another greasy Floaters burger. Besides, his father had seen him there. It was a place the guy might return to.

Instead he picked up a pair of chili dogs and a giant lemonade and settled onto a patch of sand behind one of the many beach-umbrella rental stands. He leaned his bare back against the rough plywood of the stand, keeping within the narrow band of shade that ended in a brilliant line at his toes. He gazed at the boardwalk. The last thing he wanted to look at during his break was the ocean. This was some other guard's slice of beach. Let him worry about it.

He was tired. He hadn't had more than a couple hours' sleep last night. He'd already grown so accustomed to having Kate beside him that the bed had seemed huge and empty. And Mooch, evidently respecting Kate's territory, had stuck to his rug on the floor.

Even if Kate had been there, he doubted he would have been able to sleep. Thoughts had prodded him all through the dark hours. Memories, new and old.

He had often wondered, growing up, why

his father had abandoned his family. When he was younger, the answers he'd invented were romantic. His father was a secret agent who'd left suddenly for a dangerous mission abroad. Or he had amnesia and was wandering the world lost and confused but would someday remember everything and come rushing home.

When he grew older and more cynical, Justin's explanations had changed. He'd decided that his father was a guy who'd found himself stuck with a family and a mortgage without ever really having thought it all through. He'd wanted to start over, make his life less complicated. That, Justin could almost identify with.

But the truth, as the saying went, was stranger than fiction. It had never occurred to him that far from being a secret agent, his father was just a secret . . .

His father had abandoned them for another man. It was almost funny. It *was* funny.

Justin took a sip of the lemonade, but it was too sour. Suddenly he found he had no appetite, either. He crumpled up the remains of his second chili dog and tossed it into a nearby sky blue trash can.

"Hey, good-looking," a voice called out. It took a second to recognize the voice. Chelsea was standing a few feet away, unslinging a camera bag from her shoulder.

Justin forced a smile. "Hi, Chelsea. Should you be flirting like that? You *are* practically a married woman."

Chelsea winced. "Don't start in with that, okay? I've had enough with Kate and Grace trying to turn this into the wedding of Prince Charles and Lady Di."

"Look how well that turned out," Justin observed.

"Exactly. All we wanted to do was have a little ceremony and get on with life."

Justin nodded. "Yeah, well, you do have to be a little careful about what you're planning, you know."

"Careful?" Chelsea echoed.

"The whole illegal thing."

Chelsea tried to hide her reaction. "I don't . . . what do you mean? There's nothing illegal about getting married."

"Uh-huh. Look, Chelsea, I admire the fact that you're willing to do this to protect Connor and all."

"Protect?"

Justin sighed. "Do I look that stupid? I'll admit it took a day or so for it to dawn on me, but I'm not totally dense. You think I can't guess that Connor's an illegal?" He laughed. "Every other Irishman in this town is illegal. It's an open secret."

Chelsea sagged. "So Kate knows, too?"

"I wouldn't know," Justin said shortly.

"Oh, right. I forgot you two are fighting."

"She told you we're fighting?" Justin asked.

"Didn't have to. Her bed had been slept in."

"Yeah, well, people fight," Justin said lamely.

Chelsea sat down next to him on the sand. "What did you mean, I had to be careful?"

"I meant what you're planning on doing is against the law. You know—cooking up a marriage just for the purpose of getting Connor his green card." Justin laughed at the horrified expression on Chelsea's face. "Not that they're likely to have you doing hard time in a federal prison."

"We thought this was all a great secret," Chelsea wailed. "Now the whole planet knows." She paused, frowning. "You know, we really are in love. I'd marry Connor even if he wasn't an illegal."

"I believe you," Justin said. "I just don't want to see you guys getting in any trouble." He glanced down at his watch. "Listen, I have to get back to work."

"Me too." Chelsea shouldered her bag again and stood. "I'm preserving magic memories of happy days spent at the beach."

"Never quite understood why people want to preserve memories," Justin noted dryly.

* * *

"Stop that thing with your eyes," Chelsea muttered later that afternoon.

"What thing?"

"That thing where you make them go wider," Chelsea said, moving her charcoal stick across a large sketch pad in short, quick strokes.

Connor crossed his eyes. He was sitting in a chair by the window in Chelsea's room. He wore jeans, no shirt, and an annoying cockeyed grin on his face.

"Very funny. You know, if you keep doing that, they'll stick that way."

"I thought you were drawing my newly enlarged muscles," Connor said.

"I've already done that part."

"Didn't seem to take long," Connor grumbled.

"They aren't that enlarged," Chelsea teased. "Besides, I'm marrying you for your soul, not your body."

"What's wrong with my body?"

"Nothing at all." Chelsea tilted her head sideways to look at the sketch. "At least not the parts of your body that I've seen so far."

Connor stretched out his leg and touched her foot with his toes. "I could show you—"

"Sit still," Chelsea ordered. "Now the line of your neck is different."

"Sorry."

Chelsea heard a car door slam outside, followed by a whirring mechanical noise. She jumped up from the bed to look out the window. "It's Marta. She's got one of those elevator deals on the side of her van. You know, for the wheelchair."

"Uh-huh," Connor said, not sounding too interested.

"Let's take a break," Chelsea said. "I want to go down and say hi to her."

"Um, hey," Connor said quickly. "Why not stay here with me?" He stood up and put his arms around her, kissing her softly on the lips. She tossed the sketch pad aside and ran her hands over his smooth shoulders, relishing the familiar shiver that always went through her when they touched.

"Convinced?" Connor asked.

"Try again," Chelsea responded, lacing her fingers through the thick tangle of hair behind his neck.

This time his kiss was longer, more insistent. Connor pulled her close. Their thighs and hips skimmed, his warm hands pressing at the small of her back.

"Okay, now let's go see Marta," she said, pulling away with a smile.

"Tired of me already?" Connor teased.

Chelsea trailed kisses along his collarbone.

"Never," she whispered. "But if I stay up here, I'll get myself into trouble. It's safer downstairs."

"Maybe not," Connor said.

"What do you mean? I just want to go say hello."

Connor stared out the window. "Look," he said grimly. "You can't go downstairs."

"Why not?"

"You just can't, all right?"

Chelsea stared at him, confused. She felt suddenly queasy as the realization dawned on her. "They're not doing something for me down there, are they?"

"I . . . I can't say," Connor said.

"What, a shower? A party? Oh, Lord, don't let it be a party." Chelsea moaned.

"I didn't say it was," Connor said defensively. "Just remember, you dragged it out of me. I don't want Kate and Grace angry at me."

There was a knock at the door. "Chelsea, it's Kate. Could you come out here for a minute?"

Chelsea poked a sharp finger into Connor's stomach. "I'll get you for this."

"Just play along," Connor advised.

Chelsea poked him again and opened the door. "Yes?"

"Surprise!" Kate and Grace yelled. Grace twirled a noisemaker in the air without much conviction.

"It's not my birthday, you know," Chelsea protested.

"No, it's your bachelorette party!" Kate announced proudly.

"Are there presents?" Chelsea asked, narrowing her eyes.

"No, that would be a shower," Kate said.

"Also, presents are expensive," Grace pointed out.

"Does Connor get to come?" Chelsea asked. "Or can I dump him?"

"He has his own party," Kate said. "Out in the boathouse."

"Get down here," a voice yelled up the stairwell. "Let's get this party rolling."

"Right there, Marta," Kate yelled back.

"Yeah, let's get started," Grace said. "This is my very first party as the designated driver."

Suddenly music blasted from downstairs. "I guess we'd better go," Chelsea said. "I think they're starting without us." She winked at Connor and started toward the stairs. Then she stopped, snapping her fingers.

"Oh, Connor, I totally forgot. You got a call today. An Irish girl. Named Molly or something."

fourteen

Connor popped the top from his third beer and took a deep swallow of the dark, foamy brew. No effect yet, and damn, how he wished it would take hold. Molly. Again. She had to be safely back in Ireland, didn't she? It couldn't be that she was somehow here in the States already. It was too awful to think of. What a scene she would make. She was one for scenes.

"So, Connor, you look a little down. As you should be, facing your own doom," Mick said. He was a fellow Irishman from the construction site. Three had come, along with Justin, Alec, David, and Grace's brother, Bo. All told, eight guys lounged around the boathouse, drinking various beers—sodas in the case of David and Bo. Most of the Irish contingent huddled together. Owen was deep in argument with Alec and David on the comparative merits of soccer and American football.

"Farewell to freedom," Robert said, raising

his bottle in a toast. He sat cross-legged on the wooden planks of the catwalk. Connor stood leaning against the wall, looking down at Robert and Tom. He managed a slight twisting of his lips, hoping it would pass for a smile. "Yeah, right," he said, raising his beer to take another swig.

"Hello to a green card, eh?" Tom said in a low voice.

Connor shrugged. "Maybe so."

"Well, you won't be taking her back home, now, will you?" Tom pressed. "A nice reaction you'd get to that."

"Don't start in with your racist crap again, all right, Tom?" Connor warned. "I don't have the patience."

"It's not me," Tom protested. "I've learned the error of my ways. But you'll admit she wouldn't go over too well with some of the folks back home."

Justin wandered up to their group. "I always assumed you Irish would be a little more open-minded about stuff like race," he commented.

"It's not that we're like you Americans," Robert said defensively. "We don't put sheets on our heads and burn crosses on people's lawns. It's just that we're not a multiracial society. Never have been."

"There's good and bad in both countries," Tom argued. "In Ireland you won't see girls parading around the beach half naked." He grinned wickedly. "That's one of the bad aspects of Ireland. Now, on the plus side, we aren't overrun with gangsters, unlike America. And we don't have a lot of gay people prancing around, either, acting like it's okay."

To Connor's surprise, Justin stiffened. Evidently Justin didn't take kindly to criticism of his country. Connor stifled an urge to grin. Americans—they'd criticize themselves all day and night, but heaven help the foreigner who had a bad word to say about them.

"We also don't have any jobs in Ireland," Connor pointed out. He expected the remark to calm Justin. Instead the color remained drained from his face.

"There's an old joke in Ireland," Robert said. "What's an Irish queer? A man who prefers women over whiskey."

Justin didn't smile. In fact, he no longer seemed to be hearing anything any of them said. "It's better if they're out in the open," he said in a monotone voice. "Then at least you know what they are. You don't expect one thing and . . ." He stopped, as if surprised that he was talking out loud. "I meant, you know, gays. It's better if you know. Otherwise you may go around thinking one thing, and all the time they're somebody else."

"No doubt you're right," Connor said, frowning. Justin hadn't made an ounce of sense, which was unlike him. Normally he had little to say, but he always made sense when he said it.

Justin nodded. "Well, anyway. I'm gonna go say hi to David."

Connor watched him walk away and shook his head. "Something's bothering that lad," he muttered.

There was a knock on the door, and David got up to answer it. He opened it and peeked, then closed the door again. "All right, gentlemen," David announced in a slightly embarrassed voice. "Prepare yourselves. The evening's entertainment is about to begin. Presenting . . ."

"Tell me you didn't hire a stripper." Connor groaned.

"Please. An exotic dancer." David gave him an apologetic shrug. "Alec and Justin made me do it. I was the only one with a credit card."

"It's traditional at a bachelor party," Alec explained as he cranked the volume on the stereo to its maximum.

"Bring her on," Robert yelled.

"Presenting, from Fabulous Entertainments of Ocean City, Miss . . . Talon!" David threw open the door.

Alec fell back into his seat. "Talon?"

"Well, now we're getting somewhere," Tom observed.

"Please don't let Chelsea be looking out the window," Connor muttered. "She'd never understand."

"Truth or dare?" Chelsea groaned.

"Are we sure we really want to do this, Kate?" Grace asked uncertainly. "I mean, we're getting along fine. And my experience is that suddenly blurting out the truth could leave us all snarling at each other." She sipped at a cola in a tall glass.

"Got something to hide?" Marta teased, taking a drink of her punch.

"I have plenty to hide," Grace replied. "I'm just worried I'll make you girls jealous."

"No doubt," Beth agreed.

"Let's go around in a circle," Kate suggested. She pointed at Marta. "You first. Then Grace, Beth, me, and Chelsea last because after all, she's the bachelorette."

Chelsea poured herself another glass of Kate's punch, an odd concoction that had Chelsea feeling unnaturally happy. So what if the wedding was only about sixty hours away? She was ready right now.

"Can't we just have a male stripper?" she

complained. "The guys have one down there."

"The guys have a male stripper?" Marta asked, craning her neck to see out the dining-room window.

"I have one for Marta," Grace said. "Truth or dare?"

"You don't scare me," Marta said, jutting her chin. "Truth."

"Fine," Grace said. "Are you going out with Alec for his body or his mind?"

"His mind," Marta said flatly. "I've never really noticed his body."

Everyone hooted, but Marta stood her ground. "It's true," she said. "I haven't even noticed how broad and smooth his chest is. Or how strong his shoulders are or the fact that his arms are rock hard. And I've certainly never so much as looked at that incredible butt."

"He's a definite piece of work," Grace allowed. "Although he's a bit innocent and sweet for me."

"Everyone's a bit innocent and sweet for you, Grace," Kate said. She was on her second glass of the punch, and Kate was no more used to drinking than Chelsea was.

"Justin wasn't," Grace countered, sending Kate an angelic smile.

"So," Beth said, "it would be fair to conclude

that you're going out with Alec for his body and his mind?"

"He is a little sweet and innocent," Marta said. "But that's the way I like them." She rubbed her hands together. "Now I have one for Grace. Truth or dare?"

"Oh, I'll take truth," Grace said. "A dare might involve moving, and I'm comfortable right here, watching you three get drunk on a pathetically small quantity of booze."

"Fine. I want to know, Grace—"

"My many love secrets?" Grace joked.

"No, actually. I want to know why you take flying lessons. Is it to be near David or something deeper?"

Grace glanced away for a second, her smile faltering. She clearly wasn't expecting a question that actually scratched at more than her surface. "Being around David is part of it," she admitted. "But it's not the only reason. Like, one reason is to piss my mother off. Two, because it's really fun. But mostly it's because I really like the idea of being able to fly off somewhere, far away from Ocean City."

"You sound just like Justin," Chelsea said. Then she clapped a hand over her mouth. "Not to bring up a sore topic."

"Beth's turn," Grace said with a gleam in her eye. "Truth or dare?"

"Truth. Maybe."

"Are you into David?"

Beth looked Grace in the eye. "I can honestly say no. Not that he isn't an amazing guy. He is. But I would never want to get involved with another alcoholic."

"Why not?" Grace demanded, an edge to her voice.

Beth shrugged. "Two alkies together doubles your chances for trouble, it seems to me," she said. "I'd like a boring, sensible, stable guy. A guy whose behavior I could absolutely predict, so that anytime someone asked me, 'Hey, Beth, where's Harry?' I'd be able to answer, 'Well, Donna'— Donna seems like a good name for a pushy friend—'it's Thursday night, and it's eight-fifteen, so Harry is at his weekly bowling league.'"

"Exciting," Chelsea said. Actually, it had sounded kind of nice. She'd certainly never have that with Connor. Connor wasn't the predictable type.

"Well, I've had plenty of exciting home life," Beth answered. "It's highly overrated."

"So, Kate," Chelsea said, grinning. "As your closest friend, I believe it's my job to ask the question. Truth or dare?"

"What would the dare be?" Kate asked suspiciously.

"Something very embarrassing, I assure you."

"Truth, then," Kate said. "Only remember, whatever you ask me, I can ask you harder."

"Not this, you can't," Chelsea said. "I happened to notice that for the first time in at least a week, you didn't spend last night with Justin. Trouble in paradise?"

Kate flinched and looked away. "How about a different question?"

"No, I like that question," Chelsea said.

"Me too," Grace added, smiling.

"That's private," Kate said.

Marta leaned forward in her wheelchair. "Maybe you should let Kate answer a different question, Chelsea."

Now, why is Marta defending Kate? Chelsea wondered.

"The rules of the game should be followed," Beth said. "Otherwise it isn't much of a game, is it?"

Kate blew air through her lips and nodded slowly. She cast a guilty glance toward the door. "This doesn't leave this room. Are we agreed?"

"Wow, this is going to be good," Grace said.

"No, it's not," Marta murmured.

Kate took a deep breath. "You know that Justin's father abandoned him and his mom when he was a little kid? Well, his dad is here in O.C. Justin blew him off, and I thought he should try and patch it up. Justin got mad at me, and I got mad at him back. No big deal."

"No big deal?" Grace cried. "That son-of-a-bitch father of his shows up after all these years? I'm surprised Justin didn't pound him."

"How can you say that when you don't know him?" Marta blurted. "He's a good man."

"How do you know any of this?" Grace demanded.

"That's a new question," Kate interrupted. "I answered the question Chelsea asked. So now it's my turn to ask her a question."

Kate leaned forward and fixed Chelsea with an intense gaze. "Are you marrying Connor because—"

"Hey," Chelsea interrupted. "You didn't say truth or dare."

"Okay, truth or dare?"

Chelsea allowed a faint grin to form. "Dare."

"What?"

"I choose dare," Chelsea said, enjoying the look of surprise on Kate's face.

"But I don't have a dare."

"You'll have to think of one," Chelsea said.

Kate took a sip of her punch and began nodding slowly. Her eyes narrowed. Then she told Chelsea her dare.

"But . . . but they probably won't even come up here," Chelsea protested.

"Sure, they will," Kate said. "They're drinking

beer—they'll have to pee eventually—and the only toilets are in the house."

"But . . . ," Chelsea began again.

"Yes, I think that sums it up," Beth said.

"At least we got that stripper out of there before the girls saw us," Alec said.

"What, you didn't like her?" Connor asked as he and the others climbed the steep lawn toward the house. Mooch took up the rear. "She said you were totally cut. Of course, she said it about Justin and David, too."

"I think she says it about every guy she meets," Alec said. "It seems to come right after, 'Hi, how are you?'"

"She met me," Connor pointed out. "I wasn't even partially cut, and I was the bachelor."

"The girls are going to be mad if we crash their party," Alec warned.

"Nah," Connor said. "They'll be grateful we've dropped by. Probably all sitting there bored to tears by now. Girls don't really take to the whole party concept the way men do."

"These girls are all taken, then?" Owen asked as they reached the porch.

"I know one that's taken," Connor said. The beer was finally starting to kick in. "My bride-soon-to-be."

"Awfully quiet in there," Justin observed.

"Maybe they all went to bed. All the lights are out."

"Women. No ability to party," Alec said, echoing Connor.

"All this and I don't get to meet the unlucky bride?" Owen asked.

Suddenly one shade rose in a darkened window. Then a light snapped on, revealing Chelsea, her back turned to the window. A loud crash, like cymbals sounding, and Chelsea bent forward at the waist and dropped her jeans. There were hysterical female shouts and hoots from inside, followed by chanting that sounded like, *"Moon, moon, moon . . ."*

"Ah," Connor said. "You're in luck, then, Owen. There's the future Mrs. Riordan now."

Kate waited until she was certain that the last of the guys had left the boathouse. She sat in the shadows of the front porch and watched them leave, while the moon arched overhead and began to follow the long-departed sun down toward the bay.

It had cooled, fortunately, and the night was damp and a bit chilly. The frogs were clearly audible, calling out to each other in melancholy, comic voices.

Justin came out, preceded by a bounding Mooch. Mooch paused, sniffed the air, and trotted over to greet her.

"Hi, Mooch," Kate said, stepping down onto the lawn to pat the dog. "How was the boy half of the party?" she asked Justin.

"Pretty dull stuff," Justin said. For a moment there was silence between them. "I wasn't sure you were talking to me."

"Of course I am," Kate said. "I'm mad at you. Doesn't mean I won't talk to you."

"So, how'd it go with you-all? Chelsea ready to call it off yet?"

Kate shook her head. "I thought it was all just some dumb whim at first and after she thought it over she'd realize that. But I was talking to Grace, and she said she thinks maybe Connor is in the country illegally and this is all about trying to protect him. I'm starting to think that's true."

Justin nodded, and Kate noticed he didn't seem surprised. "That's pretty much my take," he said. "Not that Connor said anything. And honestly, I do think he loves her."

"And Chelsea loves him. So I guess there really isn't anything wrong with what they're doing," Kate said reluctantly.

"Are you, uh . . ." Justin let the question hang in the air.

"That's up to you," Kate said. "I have to tell you something."

"You're not going to start up on my father

again, are you?" He shook his head angrily. "Come on, Mooch, let's go."

"Justin, there's something you don't understand."

"Come on, boy." Justin snapped his fingers, and Mooch shuffled over to his side.

"Justin," Kate called, but he was halfway back to the boathouse. "Justin, your father is dying."

Justin took two more steps and stopped.

"I just found out today—he has AIDS. That's why he came to see you." She paused. "He's saying good-bye."

For what seemed like an eternity they stood there, a few dozen feet apart, completely silent. At last Justin whispered, "Not my problem, Kate."

fifteen

"Ease up, ease up," David instructed patiently.

The nose of the plane was stuck in the air like a dolphin jumping out of water. Grace eased the yoke forward and the nose dropped, just as the last of the airspeed bled away. The plane seemed to hang motionless.

"Eerie feeling, isn't it?" David's voice, coming through the headset, was calm and amused.

The moment ended as the plane slid into a shallow dive. "That's what the start of a stall feels like," David said. "Now you know. We'll be going over various ways to avoid stalling. Do a wide left turn and head us back to the airport."

This part Grace felt she knew. Sort of. At least, she didn't worry as long as David was beside her. The plane banked left, and Grace got a clear view of the city stretched out below her. She saw miles of beach, miles of motels and high-rises and homes, and an angry red sun diving toward the western horizon, casting long shadows that obscured the busy streets.

The Ocean City Grand was passing below them. It didn't look so grand from this angle, a flat gray roof cluttered with air-conditioning machinery.

It might be her new place of employment. The night before, at the party, Kate had mentioned they were shorthanded, not that Grace couldn't have guessed that on her own. By midsummer everyone started to run a little short of help.

They hadn't promised her the job yet, but her interview this morning had gone well. How could it not go well? Grace could walk and chew gum at the same time, which put her above ninety percent of the applicants. And she knew how to project the sophisticated look they wanted at the front desk.

Whoopee. A new job.

Through the headset Grace heard David informing the tower of their approach and requesting clearance to land. She released the yoke as he took over on his side of the cockpit. The landing was smooth, as always, and they taxied to a stop at the far end of the tarmac.

"Good lesson," David said as he killed the engine.

"Am I showing real promise yet?" Grace asked.

"Well, you didn't get us killed," David joked.

They climbed out. It felt odd to be standing on hard ground again. After each lesson her legs always seemed to vibrate for a while.

"Lesson officially over," David announced. "We are no longer teacher and student."

Grace smiled coyly. "Is that supposed to mean something?"

David grabbed her hand and drew it toward him, wrapping it back around his waist and holding her close with his other hand. He leaned into her, and Grace tilted back her head, meeting his kiss.

"You doing anything tonight?" David asked huskily when they parted.

"I'm taking suggestions."

"How about going up the coast with me to a little restaurant I know and the tourists don't? And how about if we don't take your car and we do take my bike instead?"

"I like those suggestions," Grace said.

"Good. Later I'll have some other suggestions for you."

"I'll consider those, too," Grace said. When David smiled a little too eagerly, she backed away a step. "I said consider."

The ride on the big Harley was as much fun as flying. More, in a way, because she didn't have to concentrate. She only had to feel the wind whipping her hair, and smell the leather of David's jacket, and savor the feel of him in her arms. She laid her cheek against his back and watched the distances between buildings grow until soon it was all sea grass and low dunes and darkening surf, uninterrupted by anything but the occasional parked car or the infrequent serpent's coils of tumbledown wood fences that had been all but swallowed by the sand.

"You want to do something really dumb?" David yelled.

"Did you say fun or dumb?"

"Both." David slowed the motorcycle and headed onto a path through the dunes. They passed through at walking speed until they reached the harder, wet sand by the water's edge. Then David opened the throttle and they took off. Not as fast as they had traveled on the road, but it seemed a hundred times faster. The ocean was beside them, so close it looked like they were riding on its surface. Waves broke, sending churning white tongues of surf beneath them, the wheels of the bike throwing up walls of spray that settled as fine mist on Grace's face and arms.

Gray twilight was enveloping the far horizon, advancing against brilliant swirls and spears of red and orange light from the declining sun. David slowed the motorcycle and turned across the beach, powering sluggishly over the yielding dry sand. He parked the bike and helped her off.

"Why are we stopping here?" Grace asked.

"We're there," David said. He led them across the dunes, sticking to a path through the grass. The road was close by and on the road a weathered gray shack. As they got closer, Grace realized it was a tiny restaurant, a carryout place that served steamed crabs and shrimp and soda in cans. They loaded up and carried enough food for six people back to the beach.

"I'm starving," Grace admitted as they sat on the warm sand, the food spread out before them on paper napkins.

"Fresh air will do that," David said. "I hope you don't mind not going someplace fancy."

Grace looked around at the empty beach, at the gentle waves, at the first glimmering twilight stars, at the moon rising up from the sea. "This is pretty fancy," she said with a smile.

When they were done eating, they walked awhile, not talking, just enjoying the transition from day to night. The way the rhythm of the surf grew more insistent as the tide came in. The way the seagulls quieted. The way the breeze rustled the grass on the tops of the dunes.

"I mentioned I might have some other suggestions," David said.

She let him take her in his arms. "I liked your first suggestion," she said softly.

David kissed her long and deep. She returned his kisses passionately. They sank to the ground without any conscious decision. Grace lay back, looking up at a canopy of brilliant stars overhead. It was a perfect night. Peaceful, beautiful. The perfect night, the perfect place for what she knew David wanted.

What she wanted, too.

His jacket was off, spread under her head and shoulders. He leaned over her, close, and kissed her some more. Her mouth, the hollow of her throat. His hand traveled up the length of her denimed leg.

She felt herself tense beneath his touch. Her jaw was clenched. Why? It wasn't as if she had never done this before.

David seemed to sense her tension. His hand stopped moving, and his kisses softened.

Why was she feeling this way? She wanted to be with David. Had wanted to for some time. He was strong and gorgeous and smart and funny and everything she'd ever looked for in a guy.

She began to return his kisses with more fire, hoping it would carry them both away.

His fingers touched the front of her shirt. She felt the top button release. Her breathing stopped. She felt the second button, the roughness of his fingers as they touched her heart. In a second those fingers would touch her everywhere she wanted to be touched.

Everywhere *he* had touched her.

"No!" Had she spoken out loud? Yes, David was recoiling, pulling away, stunned.

Grace sat up and rebuttoned her shirt with shaking fingers.

"I thought . . . ," David said.

"I did," Grace sobbed. "I . . . I'm sorry. I just . . . can't. I want you, David, only . . ."

David took a deep, unsteady breath. "It's your decision, Grace."

Grace covered her face with her hands. "I don't know what's the matter with me. I want you. I really do, but I sort of panicked. I don't know what's wrong. I froze up inside."

David nodded slowly. "Okay."

"You're mad."

"No, I'm not," he said. Then he laughed. "I'm a little frustrated, but not mad."

"Soon," Grace promised him.

"Soon or never, Grace, I'll still love you."

The words brought tears to her eyes. They spilled down her cheeks, hot and bitter. "I wish you hadn't said that. I wish it weren't true. No, I hope it is true." She paused. "I'm just so confused."

"You don't have to say you love me back, Grace," David said softly.

"Something inside me feels dead and empty," Grace admitted.

"I know, Grace," David said. "You've lost your first and truest love. You've lost the bottle. I know."

Love? Was that what she'd felt toward booze? Desire, yes. Need, yes. A hunger that never stopped, yes.

She'd done things for it, made sacrifices for it. Given up her self-respect for it. Maybe that was a sick sort of love.

"Come on," David said, rising to his feet. "I'd forgotten how bad this time would be for you. It's not a time in my own life that I enjoy remembering."

Grace stood up. The sky was still filled with stars. The surf was still soothing. David was still David.

"Don't give up on me," Grace whispered.

"Don't give up on yourself, Grace."

sixteen

Justin opened the door carefully and slipped in on bare feet. Kate was breathing heavily, as if she were dreaming. For a while Justin stood in the dark, listening. He still wasn't sure what he was going to do, but he knew no decision would seem right unless he could talk to Kate first.

Strange, really. A few weeks ago he had made all his own decisions. It would never even have occurred to him that he would want someone else's advice or approval. He heard a change in her breathing. If she'd been having a dream, it was over now. He crept to the side of her bed and sat down on the edge. "Don't be afraid, it's me," he whispered.

He could see the whites of her eyes as she woke, confused, then recognized him. "Justin?"

"Yes. I'm sorry to wake you up, but I needed to talk."

"What time is it?"

"About two-thirty."

She sat up. "What happened?"

"Nothing." He shrugged. "Only, I've been thinking. You know, since you told me that yesterday after the party."

She put a hand on his knee.

"It's this thing about my father. I called his hotel to check, but they say he's gone."

"I know. He left yesterday afternoon. Or the day before yesterday, I guess it is now."

Justin rubbed his eyes with the heels of his hands. "I'm not sure what to do. Look, he walked out on us. That was wrong, whatever the reason. Wasn't it?"

"Of course it was."

Justin watched Kate's white curtains sweep in and out on the breeze. "You know," he said, "ever since he showed up again, ever since he admitted being gay, it seems like all I've been hearing is queer this and queer that. I never really noticed it before."

"I'm sure your father used to hear those same things, back when he was still with you and your mom," Kate said thoughtfully.

"And know the whole time that it was people like him they were talking about," Justin added. "He probably just had to take it. Laugh at the stupid jokes. I can see where that might get to you after a while. Once I started listening, it got to me pretty fast." He stroked Kate's hand.

"Last night one of Connor's Irish friends started in about gays. Queer this and that. The guy doesn't seem to like blacks much, either. It made me realize how it seems like the same people who hate gays now were busy hating blacks before them, and Jews, and whoever else there was to hate. Personally I never really thought much about them one way or the other."

Justin sighed, emptying his lungs, then breathed in deep and slow. "Anyway. I don't forgive my dad for walking away. But that's one issue. That's between him and me. The rest of it . . . him being gay, that's a separate thing. I didn't used to think it was my business, really. But when it comes to a fight between people who hate and people who are hated, I don't have much trouble deciding where I stand."

He stood up, his fingers lingering on Kate's hand. "Thanks for talking to me."

"I barely said a word," Kate said.

Justin laughed. "I guess you're right. So what do you think?"

"I think I'm proud of you." She squeezed his hand. "What are you going to do?"

"The hotel said he left a forwarding address. He's gone on to Annapolis. I thought if you'd lend me your car, I'd drive up and maybe see him."

"Of course you can take my car," Kate said. She drew him close. "Only . . . you can't leave for a while."

Grace was wide awake, staring up at the dark ceiling of her room, when she heard someone starting Kate's car. She rolled over in bed and separated the slats of the blinds. Justin. Now, why would he be taking off alone in Kate's car at three-fifteen in the morning? And he was wearing actual clothes, too. A pullover shirt and jeans. She hadn't seen him in long pants in a while.

As he pulled away, she lay back against her pillow. What a mess she'd made of the evening with David. What an idiot she must have seemed. She'd sent every wrong signal she could send. David had been right to read them the way he did. She'd been lucky he wasn't a real jerk.

Suddenly the sheets seemed clingy, and she threw them back. She stood up, her body feeling overly wired.

Her one true love was booze? What a lousy thing for him to say. Had he been trying to make her mad, get back at her for turning him down?

What a load of bull. David and Beth and all the other drunks at A.A. had distorted everything.

Talk about blowing things out of proportion. So she'd gone on a bender. Her mother pulled them about twice a month and stayed moderately drunk in between, and she seemed to be surviving.

One lousy bender. So she'd gone too far—she wasn't disputing that. She didn't want to make a habit of waking up under the boardwalk. Still, it had been a weird time in her life. A hurricane had been closing in on the town. She'd been trying to get her head straight about the fact that Justin was falling hard for Kate. And then there'd been the whole chaos of leaving her mother's home to move in here. It had been enough to make anyone go a little crazy.

Grace slipped on her robe and went out into the living room. There were no sounds from upstairs. Everyone all snug in their beds. She crept toward the kitchen.

Good old Connor, he would have something stashed away in the cupboard.

In the kitchen she snapped on the brilliant overhead light. Yellow linoleum and gleaming white counters nearly blinded her. She went to Connor's shelf in the cupboard.

Cereal, Pop-Tarts, a box of Earl Grey tea. No beer. Nothing.

Grace swallowed hard. He must have

drunk it all up with the guys at that stupid party.

She tore through the rest of the cupboards. More cereal. Macaroni and cheese. Baking soda, as if anyone in this house baked. Nothing. Not a lousy bottle of cooking sherry.

Grace threw open the door of the nearer of the two refrigerators. Milk. Orange juice. Dr. Pepper. She shoved the bottles aside angrily. Nothing behind them but some yogurts.

Her hands shook as she opened the second refrigerator. Damn it, six people kept their stuff in this kitchen and not one lousy beer?

Then she saw it. Three brown bottles. Ha, Connor was getting Americanized after all, refrigerating his beer. She lifted a bottle from the pack and carried it over to the counter. It wasn't twist off; it needed a bottle opener. The can opener, that would work, that little hook thing. She pried, once, twice, but it slipped. On her third attempt the little metal cap popped off. The smell of the rich brew. The alcohol smell of it. Her hand tightened around the bottle. It would be so good, so good, so good.

"Oh," she gasped. Her breath came in panicky gulps. The drink was right there in her hand. And there were more in the refrigerator. And more in the morning when the bars opened. And more, and more.

She set the bottle down in the sink and pulled her hand away as if it were burning. She took two stumbling steps back.

"No," she whispered, while part of her mind fed her every argument—*It won't hurt, no big deal, just one, who will know, it never killed anyone, it will settle you down, help you to sleep. . . .*

Grace shuddered and turned away. She ran blindly into the living room. She stopped, leaning heavily against the table at the bottom of the stairs. She picked up the telephone and dialed information for the number.

It took eight rings before Beth picked up the phone, her gruff voice sleepy and resentful. "What?"

"Hi, uh, Beth, it's Grace. I'm, uh . . . I guess you're wondering why I'm calling you in the middle of the night, huh?"

"No, I'm not, Grace. I'll be there in ten minutes. You can hang on that long."

The boardwalk was utterly abandoned, utterly desolate. Every shop shuttered and barred. Every restaurant closed and dark. Brightly colored bikinis looked gray in shadowed display windows, lit only by the widely spaced streetlights. The blue trash barrels had already been emptied, ready for another day. The beach had been raked clean by tractors. The ocean seemed subdued, as if it, too, were resting up for another day of hosting the tourist throngs.

It's a tired, shabby place, really, Grace thought. A place of counterfeit fun and forced hilarity. Cheap amusements for people who just wanted to forget that soon they'd be back at work, back at school, back sitting on their ratty couches, watching TV.

Grace walked along slowly, Beth next to her. They had walked a mile, heading north, with scarcely a word between them. Then, acting on some unspoken cue, they had turned back southward, past dirty display windows cluttered with postcards and beach balls and cardboard cutouts of the Bain de Soleil woman. She wouldn't be caught dead in Ocean City.

"I love this place," Beth said suddenly. It was the first sound, other than their footsteps and a distant foghorn, that Grace had heard in an hour. It seemed unreal.

"You love this place?" Grace echoed, incredulous.

"The boards," Beth said. "The boardwalk in Ocean City. I'd say someone should write a song about it, but they already wrote one about the boardwalk in *Atlantic* City."

"They have casinos, at least."

"Miss America contest, too," Beth pointed out. "But we still have them beat."

Grace let out a short laugh. "Beth, we don't have anyone beat. Three months out of the year Ocean City is a crowded, sweaty hellhole of rude tourists streaming out of tacky motels so they can spend the day blasting loud music the length of the beach and the night jostling to get to the rubbery crab legs at the all-you-can-eat buffet. The other nine months of the year it's a rainy, windy ghost town, with five thousand people rattling around in it like zombies, waiting for the season to start again."

"So you've given this some thought," Beth said dryly.

"No wonder I drink. I hate this town."

Beth shook her head. "You'd think a person with your taste in clothing—and in guys—would have more refined sensibilities." She shrugged. "I suppose it all depends on your point of view."

"You *like* this?" Grace swept her hands wide.

"I love this place," Beth said fervently. "I love it. You don't understand, Grace. Ocean City isn't like other places. Other cities are trapped in time. They don't change from year to year, let alone month to month, week to week. In other places the weather may change, but the people around you, the cars on the street, the food at the A&P, the buildings, the houses, all stay the same. Only the lighting changes.

"But here . . . each day is part of a cycle of birth and hibernation and rebirth. Each week has a significance of its own. Of course, it's a ghost town in winter and a traffic jam in summer—that's what's great. This town is always looking ahead, always waiting and anticipating. Waiting for spring because that's when we locals start to work, getting everything freshly painted and cleaned up, ready for those first tentative tourists. Then summer comes, and it's almost too much, but still, that's what we need. We need the extremism of it, the frenzy. We take it till we're exhausted and we're thinking, oh, man, I can't wait till fall when the crowds thin out, and the locals can take a day or two off every week. Finally winter. We rest. We recuperate. We get a little depressed around February or March, but by then we get to realizing that spring isn't far away."

Grace looked at Beth in surprise. "What, are you being paid by the chamber of commerce?"

Beth grinned. "Lot of locals take your attitude," she said. "You're not the only tourist hater around town."

Grace stopped suddenly, realizing where she was. Petie's bar looked different at night, with the lights off. There was the sign, though: Petie's—on the Beach.

"You know this place, I gather," Beth said.

Grace started. Had she been standing here staring for long? "It's a bar," she said.

"You used to drink here?"

"Just once," Grace said flatly. "That was enough." She realized she couldn't see the sign clearly any longer because tears had filled her eyes.

"You want to tell me what happened?" Beth asked.

Grace didn't answer. Her throat was suddenly too tight for speech.

Beth waited silently for a moment before speaking again. "You know, things always look worst at night. I believe memory is like that. I think it's the nighttime part of your brain. It casts the worst light on everything. That's why sometimes it helps a little to talk about things. You talk about them, and it's like dragging them out into the light. Embarrassing, maybe, but at least you can see things for what they are."

Grace shrugged. "I wanted a drink pretty badly."

"And . . ."

"Petie. I let him, you know . . . I let him do whatever he wanted. I let him touch me and look at me. I would have done whatever he told me to. Luckily he passed out." Grace stared bleakly at the bar.

"And it shocked you that you would do that?"

"I'm not easily shocked," Grace said with a tinge of bitterness. "More a matter of pride, I guess. I don't know what happened to me. I don't know how I could have . . ." She bit back a sob.

Beth put a clumsy hand on her shoulder and patted her softly. After a moment she turned Grace away from the bar. "Hey, look."

Grace looked up. The horizon had grown pink.

"Sun's coming up," Beth said.

"I guess it's a good thing I don't have a job to go to," Grace said. "I'd be exhausted."

"Sun coming up on the Ocean City boardwalk and a pair of tired drunks," Beth said, grinning. "Symbolic, don't you think?"

Despite herself Grace smiled back. "Did you arrange it that way?"

" 'This city now doth, like a garment, wear the beauty of the morning; silent, bare,' " Beth quoted.

"Shakespeare?"

"Wordsworth." Beth shrugged good-naturedly. "Hey, in high school, while you were sleeping with Justin, I was sleeping with Wordsworth."

Grace watched the fiery rim of the sun peek over the edge of the world and send shafts of gold against the dark. "I guess I shouldn't be depressed," Grace said. "Looks like I got the better end of that deal."

"Yeah, maybe you did, Racey Gracie." Beth raised an eyebrow. "I suppose it all depends on your point of view."

seventeen

The morning sun caught the spires of the churches and lit the white dome of the state capitol building as Justin arrived in Annapolis. He drove Kate's convertible through narrow cobblestoned streets, past quaint shops and hole-in-the-wall breakfast diners that served eggs and muffins to early rising watermen and cops going off shift.

He'd visited the town once or twice before but had never really learned his way around. Still, he knew the hotel he was looking for was on one of the two circles in the middle of the historic district.

He found himself by the dock, an area edged by trendy restaurants. Hundreds of yachtsmen and weekend sailors parked their boats there, forming a forest of tall white masts. He pulled the car over to the side and looked out at the boats. There might have been a square mile of them, from little day-trippers to sleek racing yachts to wide, comfortable catamarans.

He still wasn't sure what he planned to do next. His anger at his father hadn't lessened. And he didn't feel any particular pity for him, either. Still, if his father was dying, he deserved the minimal consideration Justin would have extended to anyone in the same circumstances.

He drove up the main street past a group of four Naval Academy midshipmen wearing U.S. Navy T-shirts as they jogged in lockstep. B. D., Chelsea's brother, was going to school here, but Justin had never met him.

At the top of the street was a circle and to the left the hotel, a historic building of red brick. The whole town seemed to be made of red brick.

Justin found a parking space down a side street and headed around back toward the hotel. While he drove, he had felt sleepy. Now he just felt tired, ragged. But awake.

The front door of the hotel opened, and two men stepped out. Justin turned instantly and ducked into a recessed doorway. One of the men was his father. The other was a younger man who walked close by his side. When Justin peeked around the corner, he saw them getting into a car with a rental-company bumper sticker. Justin trotted back around the circle to Kate's car. He pulled up the top and sank low in the driver's seat. His father would have to drive past him to exit the circle.

Justin pulled the convertible in behind the rental car as it left the circle, heading west, away from town. The street broadened, turning into a main thoroughfare. Morning rush-hour traffic was heavy, but it was all going the other way.

The rental car turned, and Justin followed automatically. They were now in a cemetery, trapped on a narrow paved path that ran between white tombstones and flat bronze markers.

The rental car parked at the top of a low hill. Justin stopped his own car several hundred feet back and watched as his father and his friend climbed out and disappeared over the hill.

Justin got out and followed, feeling sneaky and a little ridiculous as he hung back, avoiding detection behind tall marble monuments of winged angels.

His father stopped at a simple white headstone. While his friend withdrew a bit, Justin's father stood in front of the stone without moving. Justin watched, leaning against the trunk of an ancient elm.

"You look a lot like your father," a voice said.

Justin started. The other man, his father's friend, was standing beside him.

"Don't worry," he said. "Your father doesn't know you're here. I spotted you right away, though." He smiled a cold half smile. "I'm a cop. We notice things like tails, especially when the guy tailing you is in a bright red car. My name is Wayne Dannemeyer."

"Justin Garrett," Justin said. He shook the man's extended hand.

"You expected a limp wrist, I suppose?"

Justin withdrew his hand. "I didn't expect you at all. I don't have anything to say to you."

"What do you have to say to your father?"

"That's none of your business."

Wayne nodded. "You pissed at him for running out on you, for being gay, or all of the above?"

"I have nothing against . . . gay people."

"Uh-huh. But you don't like us much, either, do you?"

"I can't totally deny that," Justin admitted. "But I've thought it over and decided that I like your enemies even less."

To Justin's surprise, Wayne smiled broadly and nodded in approval. "You're honest, at least." He was silent for a while. "Although it really isn't any of my business, I think the way he walked out on you was lousy. I've told him so. And I also told him I thought he was being selfish looking you up now, dumping all this in your lap."

"Yeah," Justin agreed. "I don't even know why I came here. I'm not ready to forgive and forget."

"Look, maybe you should take off before he sees you," Wayne suggested gently. "I don't want him getting his hopes up again, and then . . ." He shrugged.

"I thought I was ready," Justin said. "But when I think of that day—" He broke off, fighting the growing lump in his throat. "I'm still angry. I was a little kid," he defended. "I didn't understand anything. I just felt like somehow it was my fault."

Wayne reached to put an arm around Justin's shoulders, then thought better of it. "Look, you know where we're staying. I'm not going to tell your dad I saw you here. You decide what you want to do. Leave me a message at the hotel. We'll be here through tonight, anyway. If there's no message . . . well, we're going to head on back to California."

Justin nodded mutely. His father was still staring down at the stone.

Without a word Justin turned and walked away.

*　　　*　　　*

Behind the altar and to the left was a stained-glass rendition of the Nativity. On the other side, the Resurrection. The altar itself was covered in brocaded white silk supporting a golden crucifix and brass candles. The carpet was a rich burgundy plush. The pews were well-aged oak. The ceiling arched high overhead, gloomy and intimidating.

The priest wore gray pleated pants and a white knit shirt that contrasted with a deep, rich tan.

It was, after all, Ocean City, Chelsea realized.

"Now, everyone just relax," Father Tom said. "This is only a rehearsal, so mistakes don't count against you. We'll get started in a few minutes."

Chelsea sent Connor a glance. He was neatly dressed, by his standards, and looking a little sick. Kate had a sullen frown. Grace yawned every few seconds. Alec winked at Marta, who rolled her eyes.

David looked around nervously. "You know, technically speaking, I don't think I'm supposed to be in here," he muttered to Grace. "If my mother saw me, she'd drop dead."

"I notice you wore your beanie," Grace said.

"Yarmulke," David said. "It's called a yarmulke. We're supposed to wear it in the synagogue, so I figured, church, synagogue, who knows? Do I wear it, or is wearing it here some kind of collaboration?"

"Nice church," Alec remarked under his breath. "Catholics have all the great churches. All we Presbyterians ever get is big barnlike places in the suburbs."

"We never went to church," Kate said. "My dad golfed, and my mom and I went to yard sales and flea markets. I never learned any Bible stories, but I can spot the difference between real Depression glass and imitation."

"I went to church," Grace said. "It gave me a solid foundation in morality so that later in life I would always know exactly which commandments I was breaking. Speaking of which, Father Tom is kind of good-looking for a priest, isn't he? What a waste."

"We had a priest when I was in L.A., you'd swear he was Christian Slater's twin brother," Marta said. "But yeah, this guy isn't bad looking, either."

"Maybe you could see if he'd like to take you to lunch," Alec muttered.

"Hey, where's Justin?" David asked.

"He had some personal business to take care of," Kate said. "He's driving to Annapolis to see his dad."

"I wish I'd thought of a good excuse like that," David said.

"All right," Father Tom said, reemerging on the platform. "I've gone over the ceremony, and I think I'm ready. Now, this is my first time, so bear with me."

"Their first time, too," Grace offered.

"Let's see, I know Chelsea is the bride, and of course I know her from Sunday mass. And the groom?"

"That would be me, Father," Connor said, holding up his hand.

"And are you and Chelsea of the same faith?" the priest asked pointedly.

"Ah, yes, that we are," Connor said.

"Funny, I don't remember seeing you at mass," Father Tom said.

"I'm often overlooked," Connor said.

"Uh-huh. Well, I'll need to have both of you into my office right after the rehearsal. I'd have insisted on it before now, only I understand we're in something of a rush, with the ceremony itself coming in less than twenty-four hours." He looked directly at Connor. "And of course, I'll expect to hear your confession."

"That ought to be good," Grace said under her breath.

"Now, who's our best man, and who's giving away the bride?"

"I thought Justin was going to be best man, the unreliable bastard," Connor said.

Chelsea poked him in the ribs with her elbow. "You're in church!"

"I didn't blaspheme," Connor said defensively. "I just said he was a—"

Chelsea poked him harder, and Connor subsided, looking wounded. "Well, who wants the job, then?"

"I'll do it," Alec volunteered. "What do I have to do?"

"You hand Connor the ring," Marta said. "Haven't you ever been to a wedding before?"

"I don't have a ring," Alec objected. "I don't have a suit, either."

"He'll give you one."

"Not a suit," Alec argued.

"The ring," Marta said. "Connor will give you the ring."

"I will?" Connor wondered. "I guess I will. I hadn't thought about it."

"You can get them on the Home Shopping Club for like twenty-nine dollars if you're one of the first ten callers," Chelsea said. "Although you need a credit card. Plus I don't know how quickly—"

"I'm getting married, and I forgot the bloody ring," Connor interrupted.

"Gee," Kate said sarcastically, "not entirely prepared for this? Who'd have ever guessed?"

"Perhaps a parent, a family member, might have a ring," Father Tom interjected.

"What family?" Kate asked. "Her family doesn't even know about this."

"You still haven't told your folks?" Marta asked.

"Why should she?" Grace countered. "Maybe her parents are jerks."

"They are not," Chelsea said, rushing to defend her parents.

"You have to tell them," Alec said. "Sooner or later."

"Later," Chelsea said. "I'll tell them when I'm ready."

"I don't see how you can not tell your parents," Alec said.

"I don't see how she can do this at all," Kate said, her voice rising. "I'm the only atheist here, and *I'm* the one who thinks this is immoral."

"You're an atheist?" the priest asked, looking shocked.

"Maybe you can save her," Grace said sincerely.

"I get the feeling Grace is feeling better," Connor whispered in Chelsea's ear. "I haven't seen her this fired up in a while."

"I know, and I wish she would stop," Chelsea whispered back. "Is it just me, or is this thing not off to a good start?"

"You want to back out?" Connor asked.

"You know you can at any time, though time is getting rather short."

Chelsea sighed. "Of course not. Once we get through this rehearsal, I think everything will be fine. *If* we get through this rehearsal."

eighteen

"Well, that was pleasant," Connor growled, throwing himself down on the end of Chelsea's bed. "The rehearsal from hell, followed by thirty minutes of 'counseling' from that young whelp of a priest, a man not five years older than me and a whole lot less experienced. Fortunately I was able to give him a somewhat condensed version of confession."

Chelsea sat in the chair by the window and gripped the arms tightly. "You know, I really thought Kate would support me in the end, not make sniping remarks from the sidelines."

Connor waved his hand in the air. "Ah, don't blame Kate. She's only trying to look out for you. And after all, this must seem bizarre at best."

"Bizarre?" Chelsea tried out the word, not liking it.

Connor sat up. "One day you and Kate are traipsing off to Ocean City for a summer of good times and fun on the beach, and the next minute you're getting married to a man you didn't even know six weeks ago."

Six weeks? Had it really been that short a time? Chelsea marveled. Not *even* six weeks.

"Plus," Connor went on, "you're keeping it a secret from your parents, your brother, everyone back home. You're marrying a white guy, a fellow who's not even an American."

"What are you saying?" Chelsea asked.

"Nothing. Except don't be too hard on people for thinking we're nuts. By all normal standards, we are."

Chelsea realized her fingernails were digging into the arms of the chair. She released her grip. "Maybe I should tell my parents."

"You wouldn't want them bursting into town followed by a platoon of lawyers looking for an annulment. Would you?" Connor asked.

"No, that's right. That's exactly what my dad would do. And my brother, B. D., would probably beat you up."

Connor winced at the prospect.

Chelsea sighed. "Connor, do you realize how little we even know about each other?" she said. "I mean, I don't know your middle name."

"Duke," Connor said promptly. "My dad was a big John Wayne fan. Loved the Duke. The last real movie star, according to him."

"I don't know what your favorite color is, or your favorite music, or how you feel about the major issues of the day—"

"Red, the blues, and Brits out of Ulster."

Chelsea stared at him, feeling dissatisfied and annoyed without knowing why. "What's *my* favorite color?"

"Yellow?"

"Blue. What kind of music do I like?"

"Jazz? Rap?"

"Jazz makes me nervous, and rap is too heavy. I like reggae and Motown and the blues, same as you." She thought for a moment, all the while keeping her gaze fixed on Connor. Connor began humming the tune from *Jeopardy!*

"Very funny," Chelsea said. "Okay, relatives for a hundred. What does my mom do for a living?"

"What is publishes a magazine?"

"Okay, you remembered that," Chelsea said. "Try this. Favorite movies for three hundred—what's my favorite horror movie of all time?"

"Um, what is *Friday the Thirteenth? Part Two? Part Three? Part Four?*"

"Trick question. I hate horror movies."

Connor sighed. "You think a marriage is built by being able to answer a bunch of trivia questions? Do you think Jennifer Aniston knows Brad Pitt's favorite color? Do you think Fred Flintstone knows Wilma's favorite movie?"

"You put an actor and a cartoon character in the same example?"

"I was having a hard time thinking of successful marriages." Connor laughed, then grew serious. "Look, we both know what this is about. I love you, you love me."

Chelsea sighed again. "You're right. I guess Father Tom got to me with all that stuff about sacraments and sacredness. It's just that, you know, we're just eighteen. Eighteen! I have a high school diploma in a country where I need a college degree to flip burgers. I've only been driving for like two years, and I'm not very good at it. I don't know how to cook anything but Kraft macaroni and cheese. What makes me think I know enough to jump into something that's so *permanent?*" The word made her shudder. "It's like I've decided to have plastic surgery or get tattooed. Except I would put more thought into those things."

Connor stood up suddenly and began pacing back and forth. "Look, Chelsea, I can't answer any of that. I have no answer! What can I say? I've got a conflict of interest, don't I? I'm the one looking at deportation, not you, and I haven't asked you, and I won't ask you, to do this for me. It wouldn't be fair or right. I think maybe we should call this off now, before it goes any further. I don't want to spend years, or the rest of our lives, or whatever it turns out to be, with you thinking I used you for my own purposes."

Chelsea recoiled. What was he saying? What did he really want? "You think I'll hold this against you?"

Connor threw up his hands. "You keep talking, and that silly priest kept talking, in such apocalyptic terms. Forever and ever. Till death parts us. Me, I don't think in those terms. I don't know what I'll be doing a month from now, let alone for the rest of my life. You're right, Chelsea, I'm just eighteen myself. A child. A poor lad trying to climb that next rung on the ladder without slipping and breaking his silly neck."

"But if we get married, we're making a sacred vow before God," Chelsea argued.

"That's why there's confession and redemption, eh? So that when we screw up and fall on our asses, we can climb back up and have another go."

Chelsea sank back in her chair. "So you're already planning for this marriage to fail?"

"No, Chelsea," Connor said, his voice more gentle. "I'm planning for us to love each other forever. To have earthshaking sex. To raise a handsome family. For you to become a famous artist and me a famous writer. I'm planning an attractive, roomy home on the ocean with a study where I can write and at the end of the day you'll come in and sit on my lap and tell me you've sold another painting for half a million dollars and oh, by the way, the teacher says little Johnny's a prodigy. That's my plan."

"That's a good plan," Chelsea said softly.

"Yes, and all that stands in the way are the Immigration Service, your friends and family, my friends and family, the law of averages, the rules of probability, rising property values, falling meteors, earthquakes, car accidents, taxes, disease, famine, pestilence, war, and any other Horsemen of the Apocalypse I may have forgotten, plus every racist in the world." His voice rose, then fell. "So my point is, forever is a very long time."

"Forever," Chelsea repeated. "Or at least till you get a green card, and then, I guess, we'll take the rest a little at a time."

"Yeah." Connor seemed deflated. "I guess we'll see."

Kate knocked tentatively at the boathouse door, then opened it.

Justin was sitting on the deck of his boat,

using a short piece of rope to play tug-of-war with Mooch.

"Hi," Kate said. "I saw the car, so I knew you were back."

Justin gave her a tired smile. "It's almost out of gas. I'll fill it up for you tomorrow. How'd the rehearsal go?"

Kate shook her head. "Too bad you missed it. One of the better displays of fireworks I've seen. Of course, it could have gone worse. Could have if we'd invited, say, a couple dozen Hell's Angels and a pack of snarling wildcats."

Justin laughed loudly, which brought a reluctant smile to Kate's lips. "I was a bitch. So was Grace. I think our clever plan to make Chelsea reconsider is about eighteen hours away from major failure."

"She's doing what she thinks is right," Justin said.

Kate sighed as she joined him. "Yeah, I know. That makes it hard to really argue with her. How did it go with you?"

Justin's smile disappeared. He let Mooch take the rope away. "I didn't speak to my father," he admitted. "I talked to his . . . you know, his friend." He held up his hands in a gesture of helplessness. "I liked the guy. We talked. I'm supposed to let him know if he should drag my dad back to Ocean City for one last go-round."

"And?"

"And I don't know." He looked up at her, his eyes full of confusion. "I mean, what's the deal here? I'm the victim. I'm the one who got hurt because of what he did. Why the hell is it my job to forgive and forget?"

Kate thought the question over for a moment. She sat down on the floor in front of him, letting her hand settle on Mooch's head. "I don't know, Justin. But when you think about it, who else *would* be in the business of forgiving but a victim? That's pretty much the definition of the word, isn't it?"

"So I get the suffering, and then I have to forgive, right? Does that seem fair?"

"Not really, no," Kate admitted.

Justin clenched his teeth. "If he weren't dying, I'd tell him to drop dead." Then he rolled his eyes. "That makes a lot of sense."

"I don't think you should forgive him just because he's sick," Kate said.

Justin blinked. "You don't?"

"In a way it's not really the point."

"It's the only point for me," Justin said. "If I thought he was going to live another twenty years, I wouldn't even consider this. I hate the man. He's the only person on earth I can honestly say I hate."

Kate leaned close and wrapped her arms

around his neck, drawing their heads together. "You don't hate him. That would have been a lot easier than what you really feel. I think the truth is he's still your dad and you still love him."

Justin was silent. He looked down at the ground. "I *want* to hate him," he said at last in a strangled voice.

"I know," Kate said. "But that's not the kind of person you are. I don't think you'll ever be very good at hating. If you were, I wouldn't be in love with you."

Justin looked away. "I guess I could show him my boat," he said. "He'd probably like that."

"Probably," Kate agreed.

Justin climbed to his feet. "I better get to work, then. The forward cabin's a mess."

nineteen

Her hair was touched with gray over her right temple. She was wearing glasses, pushed down on her nose so she could peer over them. On her lap she held a wide book, richly bound, the colors vivid and slick. The name of the book was *My Famous Stuff*.

Chelsea wondered who the woman was, smiling at her knowingly. She looked familiar, sort of like her mother, sort of like her grandmother. She looked more closely at the cover of the book and read the author's name— O'Chelsea O'Lennox-O'Riordan.

Me, Chelsea thought, surprised at the realization. *Me, only older.*

Oh, so it was a dream. Of course. In real life she didn't wear glasses.

There was someone standing in a doorway, looking on. A middle-aged man, lit by a golden light, his smile mischievous. "See?" he said. "See? You won Final Jeopardy."

Chelsea glanced around the room, looking for his book. She saw a poster—an advertisement for an amazing-looking car.

"Advertising," the man said with a quirky grin. "Not poetry, advertising. Who knew?"

"Bye," Chelsea said, waving. "I have to go now."

"We know," the woman said.

"Bye."

Bye.

Chelsea woke gently, the dream still vivid in her mind, a soft, warm glow of contentment. Connor and her, a long time from now. Happy. Together.

"A definite improvement over the last dream I had," she said aloud. She threw back the covers and turned off her alarm clock. It wouldn't go off for another twenty minutes, but she was awake now. She was incredibly awake.

She went to the mirror on her closet door and looked at herself. "At least you didn't get fat," she told her reflection. "And you could always dye that gray."

She turned away, grabbed her robe, and headed out in the hall toward the shower.

"That was my last night of sleep as a single person," she said. The thought sent a wave of sadness over her, but it was quickly washed away by the sweet glow from the dream.

"Everything's going to be all right," Chelsea said.

"Go-in' to the chap-el . . ."

Grace sang an exaggerated version of the 1950s tune while straightening the collar on her dove gray linen suit. She winked at Chelsea. "Hey, you look great. Shouldn't you be wearing white, though?" She winked again. "Extra-virginal white?"

Chelsea shook her head. Grace's spirits had definitely picked up lately. She was back to being her usual sardonic, provocative self. Just what Chelsea didn't need.

"I don't have anything white," Chelsea admitted. "Or cream, or even beige." She twirled for Grace's benefit. "In fact, this is the closest thing I have to something formal." It was a black dress, cut low in the front. "I figure with this velvet jacket it doesn't look too sleazy."

"You could have borrowed something from me," Grace suggested.

Chelsea smiled sweetly. "I'm afraid everything of yours would have been too small in the bust."

Grace clapped a hand to her chest. "Ooh, right through the heart. A little touchy, are we?"

"I'm fine, actually," Chelsea said. Her ankles wobbled on her high heels. "By the way, when do people start going gray, do you think?"

There was a clatter of footsteps on the stairs, and Kate came rushing down. "Are you two ready? Wow!" She gave Chelsea a thumbs-up. "Las Vegas bride."

"A sexy little number," Chelsea said. "Perfect for a night on the town or a holy sacrament."

"Straight from the wedding ceremony to the honeymoon without changing," Kate joked. She came closer, and Chelsea could see her eyes were moist.

"Look, Chels, you know how I feel about you doing this," Kate began. She put her hand on Chelsea's arm. "But if you're going through with it, I'm still your friend and always will be. You know I love you."

Chelsea felt her lip begin to quiver. "I know, Kate," she said. "I know you were doing what you thought was right."

"Oh, you can count on Kate for that," Grace said, gently mocking. "Just like you can count on me."

"To do what's wrong?" Kate said.

"Absolutely." Grace nodded.

"I had a dream last night that it was all going to work out fine. I'll be a famous artist, and we'll live in a house with really bad wallpaper. I don't know why the wallpaper's bad, but I think maybe it's the style in the future."

Kate came forward and gave her a long, hard hug. "Friends forever, all right?"

"Absolutely," Chelsea said.

"I had a dream last night about that guy in the Obsession cologne ads—" Grace began.

"Come on, Grace, group hug," Chelsea interrupted.

"Do I have to?" Grace moaned, putting her arms around Chelsea.

The front door opened, and Justin walked in with Alec. "Quick, turn around," Justin muttered. "They're weeping and hugging."

"It was inevitable," Alec said. "And there's bound to be more before this thing is done."

"Hey, Chelsea," Justin said, "when is it I get to kiss the bride?"

"When she's not a bride anymore," Kate said. "But you can kiss the bridesmaid now."

"Is this okay?" Alec asked, looking down at his cotton pants and white oxford shirt. He stuck out one leg. "I didn't have any socks. Neither did Justin."

"You look great," Chelsea reassured him. "We're going to be a pretty motley-looking crowd."

"Hey, can I come down?" Connor yelled from upstairs.

"Sure," Chelsea said.

"No!" Kate shouted. "You're not supposed

to see the bride before the wedding. It's bad luck."

"Really?" Chelsea asked.

"Look, you're getting married. Don't tempt fate by ignoring any more traditions than you absolutely have to."

Kate yelled back up to Connor, "Justin's back with my car, so you and the guys go in Alec's car."

"Marta's going to pick up Beth," Alec said.

"David's meeting us there," Grace confirmed.

"Then I guess it's time," Chelsea said. She gulped.

"Are you scared?" Grace asked.

"I'm so nervous, I'm sick," Chelsea admitted. "I'll probably hurl in the middle of the whole thing."

"You won't," Kate assured her. "You'll be fine. Alec, do you have the ring?"

Alec felt in his pocket. "Yeah. I'm all set."

"Okay," Kate said. She sent Chelsea an inquiring look, a look that asked if she really wanted to go through with this.

Chelsea started to answer, but her mouth was dry. She nodded mutely. She turned and headed for the door on legs that had suddenly gone numb.

*　　*　　*

"So can I come down now?" Connor called. He had heard the girls leaving, but he didn't want to take any chances on getting yelled at. His nerves were stretched tightly enough. He'd barely slept, tossing and turning and drifting in and out of weird, fantastic dreams.

"Come on down, you poor dumb sucker," Alec replied.

Connor shakily descended the stairs. What a cliché. The nervous bridegroom.

Justin was there, dressed in clean blue jeans and a white button-down he'd probably borrowed from Alec. Alec was using the remote control to flip idly through TV channels with the sound off.

"You look lovely," Justin said dryly.

Alec snapped off the TV. He smirked at Connor. "A tweed jacket, and it's what—about ninety-three degrees out there? Good fashion choice."

"It'll be fine," Connor grumbled. "I'm in a cold sweat as it is. The last thing I'll have to worry about is being hot."

"You know, the girls had a big group hug," Alec suggested.

"Not bloody likely," Connor said. "How did Chelsea seem?"

"Looked pretty sexy, actually," Alec said. "Better than you. Don't you have a tie, at least?"

"A tie?" Connor echoed. "I spent thirty-two bucks on that ring you're holding, a hundred and twenty on a hotel room for tonight so I don't have to worry about you louts down here giggling while Chelsea and I enjoy our first night as man and wife. I should spend another twenty on a tie?"

"What a sentimentalist," Alec joked.

"It would have been a waste of time," Justin said. "We don't allow ties in Ocean City. Under O.C. rules, a long-sleeved shirt is the equivalent of a tuxedo."

"Well, we better get going," Alec said, glancing at his watch.

"Can I have a good strong drink first? Or maybe six?"

"Oh yeah, that would be a great idea," Justin said. "Come on, boy. It's too late to bail out now."

Connor nodded stiffly. Yes, it was finally too late to bail out. It was going to happen. It was actually going to happen.

He should be feeling elated.

Outside, the morning sun was shining weakly, but the air was already muggy and oppressive. They walked like a funeral procession toward Alec's Jeep.

"Want me to drive?" Justin said.

Alec gave him a murderous look. "The last

time you drove, it resulted in twelve hundred dollars in repairs. When my dad realizes how much his insurance rates are rising, I'm going to tell him to look for you."

The engine roared to life, and Alec made a U-turn, sliding past a yellow taxi that was creeping tentatively down the street.

"Enjoy the ride," Alec advised. "Once you're married, you're required to buy a minivan."

Connor's face was too stiff for him to grin. Suddenly he heard what sounded like someone calling his name. He turned, but all he saw was the taxi flashing by as Alec pressed on the gas pedal.

Now I'm imagining things, he told himself. *Hearing voices. Please don't let me pass out or puke. Or at least if I do, let it be after I've said, "I do."*

twenty

"Maybe he won't show up. I mean, he might decide not to do this and just drive off with the guys," Chelsea chattered. "I mean, who knows? It's not like I can totally predict everything he'll ever do. Is it cold in here?"

"No, it's not cold," Kate said.

"I guess you're right," Chelsea said, glancing around at the small room. The walls were cracked white, and the edges of the ancient woodwork were rounded off by dozens of coats of paint.

"Are you ready?" Kate asked.

"Uh-huh," Chelsea lied.

"Do you remember everything you're supposed to say?" Grace asked.

"What?" Chelsea answered, having trouble hearing anyone over the sound of her racing heartbeat.

"The rehearsal, girl. Focus. Do you remember the rehearsal?"

"Kind of," Chelsea said. "There was a lot of arguing, right?"

"Yes, that was the rehearsal," Grace answered. "Kind of a warm-up for married life."

"What? Did you say something?" Chelsea asked.

"No. Not a word."

"Any minute now," Kate said. "Just be cool. The organ will start playing, then we go. Are you all set?"

"The organ?"

"You know, the 'Wedding March.'"

"My mom is going to kill me."

"Don't worry about all that right now."

"I'm wearing an evening dress!" Chelsea moaned. "I'm showing cleavage!"

"Hey, it's Ocean City, remember?" Grace soothed. "The priest will be happy you're wearing shoes."

"Look, I think I know why you're doing this, Chelsea," Kate said. "And—"

"Why?" Chelsea demanded in a panic.

"To help Connor," Kate said calmly. "That's right, isn't it?"

"I . . . I . . ."

"I think it's a noble thing," Kate said. Then under her breath she added, "Dumb, but noble."

"She's standin' by her man," Grace commented.

Suddenly Chelsea heard a loud sound.

"What's that? What's that?" Chelsea cried.

"That's the organ," Kate said in a low voice.

"I'm not ready," Chelsea said desperately, patting her hair and pulling at the hem of her dress.

"You look great," Kate reassured her.

"I don't—"

"No, it's supposed to be 'I do,' Chelsea," Grace said.

"My legs don't work," Chelsea said. She had commanded her feet to move, but they seemed glued to the floor.

"You can still back out," Kate said softly.

"I'm only a child," Connor said. "I've barely begun to live. And now . . ." He looked around the tiny, stifling room as if it were a prison cell. There was no air.

"Marriage isn't *quite* the same as death," Justin said.

"Close," Alec allowed, "but not quite as painful."

"This is all so . . . I didn't think I'd be this . . . I mean, it was supposed to be no big thing."

"Marriage? No big thing?" Justin drawled. "What would it take to qualify as a big thing in your book?"

"I mean, well, it's all so permanent. A permanent solution to—" He fell silent, glancing suspiciously at Alec and Justin. Then he hung his head. "I mean, I love her, but there are other things pushing us to get married. Selfish things."

"Oh, really?" Justin rolled his eyes. "Naturally, Alec and I have no idea what you're talking about. You know, given that we're both a couple of idiots who just fell off the back of a turnip truck."

"You know, then?" Connor asked. He should have been annoyed, or at least paranoid, but he felt relieved. "You weren't supposed to know. It was for your own good."

"I think everyone has figured it out by now," Alec said. "Except maybe for the priest."

"He knows, too," Connor said. "He heard my confession."

"And he didn't object?"

"Father Tom O'Flannery, whose own grandfather and grandmother were immigrants?" Connor shrugged. "He objected for the record, so to speak. But I think there was so much else in my confession that he felt this was the least of it."

"So?" Justin asked. "Why the cold feet?"

"You say you love Chelsea, she loves you," Alec pointed out. "You probably shouldn't be getting married, but hey, no one wants to see you get kicked out of the country, either."

Connor winced. "It's like I'm using her to protect myself, you understand? It's . . . it's dishonorable." He laughed. "And that's not a word I use every day."

"Look, you do it or you don't," Justin said. "No middle ground on this."

"I'm going to do it, but I'm not feeling good about it." Connor screwed up his face. "I think I'm actually feeling guilty."

"A first, huh?" Justin said, smirking.

"Yeah. I don't think I've ever felt guilty before."

"I cheated on a social-studies test in seventh grade," Alec said. "I felt guilty about that. I still do."

"You gangster, you," Justin teased.

Suddenly there was a loud, vibrating sound that made the walls rumble.

"That's either your cue or we're having an earthquake," Alec said. "I have the ring. Go out there and get the finger."

"What if I never get over feeling guilty?" Connor asked desperately. "I'm not equipped to cope with it."

"I'm not going to shove you out there," Justin said. "Your call."

"Chelsea might kill you, but you could still back out," Alec said.

*   *   *

Move your foot, Chelsea commanded herself. *The foot moved. Okay, now the other one. Good. Now there's the door. Good. Now Kate is holding it open. There's David! What's he doing here? Oh, right, he's giving me away.*

My dad should be doing this, not David. What's with his arm? He's holding it crooked.

"Take his arm," Kate whispered in her ear.

Oh. Of course. Chelsea laid her hand on his arm. He smiled, and she felt her stomach swim. *No, don't puke on David, he's the best-dressed person here.*

Okay, okay, we're walking. Fine, that's easy. Okay, we're walking, and there's the aisle. Walking down the aisle. That's the phrase, isn't it? Walking down the aisle.

Father Tom. He's smiling. That's good. He doesn't hate my dress. Someone up there sitting outside the pew. Right in my way! Get out of . . . oh, it's Marta. Oh, good, I'm glad she's here. She's very sensible. She won't let anything stupid happen. Like a marriage, for example.

Where's Kate? Oh, I looked back. You're not supposed to look back, you're supposed to be radiant. Smile. No, don't smile, you'll get sick.

Who are all these people? I don't know all these people. Connor's friends from work? People from my work? Maybe that's who they are. I only see them in bathing suits or shorts. No bathing suits in church.

We're almost there! There's Connor. He looks pink. Justin and Alec are there, too. Maybe Kate will marry Justin. Wait, we could stop this and get married together. That would be so great.

Mom is going to kill me. Then B. D. will kill me. Daddy will just shake his head. Shake, shake, shake, and I'll cry.

Don't think about crying. Are we there yet? Don't look at Father Tom. Don't look at the cross. Don't look at Connor.

No, you moron! Don't close your eyes, you're still walking.

Just say, "I do." That's it, that's all you have to say: I do. Hell, any idiot can manage that, right? Take her hand, blah blah blah with the priest, then the big "I do," and bang, you're married and half of everything you own belongs to her. Instantly.

Not that I own anything. My clothes. My books. She wouldn't want those, would she?

At least we'll get to have sex. Concentrate on that. Sex and a green card. Sex and a green card.

Wonderful, Connor! Just the sort of thoughts you should be having in a church, with the boy priest not five feet away and stained glass all around. I'll be cursed for sure now.

I do love her, though. Don't I? Well, how should I know? If we don't know, who does, eh?

We're talking to ourselves. We? There's only one of us in here, you damned fool. So shut up.

"Dearly beloved, we are gathered here . . ."

It's starting, Chelsea realized. *It's actually happening. It's happening right now.*

Surprisingly, she felt her fear begin to drain away. She stole a glance at Connor and caught his eye. His death-mask rigidity slowly gave way to a smile. He sent her a look that said, "Well, here we go."

"Who gives this woman?" Father Tom asked.

"I do," David answered. He stepped back and away.

Amazing, Chelsea thought. *I'm getting married. In a minute, less even, I'll be a married woman. And it's okay, really.*

"If anyone should know just cause why these two should not be joined in holy matrimony . . ."

No, Chelsea thought, *no reason why we should not.*

". . . let him speak now or forever hold his peace."

From somewhere came the sound of a throat clearing.

Chelsea kept her eyes glued on Father Tom. He was looking rather startled.

"Actually, Father," said an unfamiliar woman's voice, "I believe that I do."

"Excuse me?" Father Tom said, gaping.

"I believe that in the eyes of God, Connor Riordan is already married," the voice said, gaining strength. Chelsea recognized the accent—just like Connor's. A cold fear traveled through her body.

"Molly!" Connor hissed.

Chelsea turned around and stared at the pretty girl with long blond hair. She was holding an infant, wrapped in a fuzzy blanket.

"You see, he's the father of our little girl," Molly said in her lilting Irish accent.

Connor let loose a word that had probably never been heard inside the church before.

Kate gasped. Father Tom started turning red. Grace let out an awed, "Wow."

"This isn't supposed to happen," the priest complained, sounding bewildered. "I don't know what to do."

"Call a time-out," Justin suggested under his breath.

"Um, there will be a brief intermission," the priest announced.

"During which there will be a murder," Connor muttered.

Chelsea felt her head swimming. Her knees were buckling. She caught a glimpse of David making a lunge toward her.

Then she hit the plush burgundy carpet.

twenty-one

They were back in their living room. Back in what should have been safe, familiar territory for Chelsea. Only there was a strange young woman sitting across from her, and a child with tiny pink hands clasping and unclasping and gurgling.

Chelsea's own hand was clasping and releasing in much the same way. Kate held on to it, sitting close beside her on the couch. Connor paced the room, playing to the occupants of the two couches like they were the two sides of an audience. Everyone else had wisely disappeared after leaving the church in disarray.

"That is *not* my child," Connor said, waving his arm wildly. "Even if it were, that does *not* mean we're somehow married."

"I didn't say it was legal, did I?" Molly asked. "Only that it was a marriage in the eyes of God."

"I didn't know you were on such close

terms with the Almighty, Molly," Connor said with a sneer. He pointed at the infant. "It doesn't even have my hair or my eyes."

"It?" Molly shot back harshly. "This is a little person, Con, not an object. Her name is Connie."

"Connie," Connor repeated. "What a nice touch. And are you claiming her last name is Riordan, too?"

"I don't know why you're acting this way," Molly said. "I'd have thought you'd be proud to be the father of a beautiful little girl." The baby began to fuss noisily. Molly held her close, gently patting her back. She turned to Chelsea and said, "She needs to be burped a lot. She's a bit dyspeptic, like her father."

"For all I know, her father is the milkman or the postman," Connor said angrily.

"Could she be yours?" Chelsea asked in a whisper.

Connor looked at her blankly.

"I mean, you know," Chelsea said. "Did you two . . ." She motioned toward Molly.

Connor sighed. "We had a relationship, if that's what you're asking. Yes. But we were always careful."

"Not always," Molly corrected.

"Every bloody time," Connor nearly shouted. "Because I didn't want you pulling a stunt like this."

Molly smiled at Chelsea. "He never was one for commitment. I was quite surprised to find him ready to take the plunge with you. If you don't mind my asking, are you pregnant by him as well?"

"No," Chelsea said sharply. "Of course not."

Molly looked at her with doubt in her light eyes. "Are you certain?"

"I'm absolutely certain," Chelsea said hotly.

"Ah, so you're a good girl, then," Molly mocked.

"That's right, Molly, she is," Connor said firmly.

Molly shot him a look. "I didn't know you were so keen on good girls. You took quite a different attitude with me, didn't you? Many, many nights, and some days as well, you took quite a different attitude. In fact, if you'd been all that keen on me being a *good* girl, I wouldn't be sitting here, rocking your baby on my lap."

"Not mine," Connor said stubbornly.

"It should be easy enough to check out with a simple blood test," Kate cut in.

Chelsea thought she caught a flicker of worry in Molly's eyes. Then again, maybe Chelsea was seeing what she wanted to see.

"I don't need a test to be sure," Molly said. "I know who I was with and when."

"You must be keeping quite a list," Connor snapped.

The baby began to wail. Molly narrowed her eyes at Connor. "Now look what you've done."

"Molly," Connor began in a more gentle tone, "what is it you hope to accomplish? Other than ruining my life. You fly here to America with an infant child and no one to care for it. At least at home you'd have your folks to help out."

"A child needs her father," Molly said stubbornly.

"If you imagine that I'm some sort of millionaire because I'm living in America, you're dead wrong. I'm barely making ends meet. I have trouble enough supporting myself, let alone a baby."

Molly looked at him slyly. "And still you were ready to marry this person." She pointed at Chelsea.

"*This* person doesn't have a baby and doesn't need to be supported," Chelsea said, resentful at being pointed at like an object. After all, this was her house, not Molly's. And Connor was her boyfriend, almost husband, not Molly's.

And he wasn't the baby's father. Probably. At least, she had to take his word for it, didn't she?

"No offense, love," Molly said kindly. "I know how much of a shock this must all be to you. And I am sorry about ruining a day you must have been looking forward to." She turned back to Connor. "And you're wrong about me depending on you, Con. I have my mother's sister and her husband living in New York. He's an American and makes a lot of money in banking. I was going to take myself and the baby there, only I want the baby's father, too."

"I'm not taking off to New York with you," Connor said.

Molly sighed. "You just need some time to adjust to the idea, that's what you need."

"I think what I need here is what Kate suggested, a blood test." Connor nodded thoughtfully. "If I'm the baby's father, well . . . that's one thing. I'll deal with that if I have to. If I'm not, then there's no problem, is there?"

"You are," Molly said softly.

Was that sincerity in her eyes, Chelsea wondered, or was she a good actress?

"Can I use your bathroom?" Molly said, brightening suddenly.

"Through there." Kate pointed.

Molly kissed the baby and held it out toward Connor.

"I don't want it," he said, pulling back.

"I can't take her into the bathroom with me," Molly insisted. "She doesn't bite, you know."

Connor's features drew together in disgust. Reluctantly he held out his arms and took the bundle of blankets. "What do I do with it?" he asked.

"Hold on to her and let nature take over." Molly smiled wistfully and headed toward the bathroom.

As soon as she was gone, Kate leaned toward Chelsea. "I think she's lying," she said.

Chelsea's eyes widened. She wasn't even sure what to believe. How could Kate sound so confident? "Why would she lie?" Chelsea asked.

"Oh, so now you believe her?" Connor demanded.

"You did sleep with her," Chelsea said in an accusing tone.

"It was a long time ago," Connor said. "It's not like I was being unfaithful to you."

"I'm just saying it's possible, isn't it?"

Connor started to answer, then seemed to collapse inward. "Maybe it is," he said bleakly. "Although I was far from the only one."

Chelsea covered her face with her hands. "I had a dream all this was going to work out," she said. "So much for dreams."

Connor came over and put his hand on her head. "It will still work out, Chelsea. Some way or other."

Right, Chelsea thought. It was all going so well. An illegal alien with an illegitimate child. Exactly what she'd always hoped for in a husband.

She got up and walked over to the porch window. It was turning out to be a bright, sunny morning. She should be married by now, worrying about and looking forward to her first night with Connor. Or she should at least be working, out walking the beach, taking pictures in a simpler life that seemed now like a long time ago. As she stood watching, a middle-aged guy in a baseball cap crossed the lawn, heading for the boathouse.

"Look," Kate said in her no-nonsense voice, "when Molly comes back out, we insist on a blood test. It's quick and sure." She paused. "Speaking of which, what's taking her so long in there?"

Connor shrugged. Then Chelsea saw a look of alarm in his eyes. "Damn!"

Kate jumped up from the couch. "I'll go see," she said, and bolted toward the bathroom.

"What's going on?" Chelsea asked, bewildered.

She heard Kate knocking on the bathroom door. "Molly?" she called. Then, more forcefully, "Molly, are you in there?"

"Damn that girl!" Connor snapped. He started to run, then realized he was still holding the baby and stopped in confusion.

Chelsea heard Kate opening the bathroom

door. There was a long silence before she reappeared. "The bathroom window is open. And Molly's not in there."

"You just need some time to adjust to the idea," Chelsea quoted. She looked at Connor, who was staring down in horror at the baby. "There isn't that much time in the world."

Justin opened the door and stood back awkwardly. His father stepped in, looking tentative and hopeful. Justin turned away immediately and crossed to a plastic foam cooler on a workbench. He reached in and held up a can of soda.

"Want a Coke?"

"I am a little thirsty," his father admitted.

They each opened a can and took several swallows. To Justin the silence seemed to stretch between them forever.

"This your boat?" his father asked.

Justin nodded. "Yeah. I bought it as pretty much a bare hull."

"Yeah?"

"Uh-huh. I, uh, I overhauled the engine."

"What do you have in there?" his father asked, taking another sip.

"They call it a Volvo Saildrive," Justin said. "Ever see one?"

"I have a little sixteen footer," his father said. "I've got an outboard on it." He shrugged.

"Not a real yacht, like this boat of yours."

For some reason Justin felt his throat tightening up. He nodded in response.

"Mind if I go aboard?" his father asked.

"It's kind of a mess still."

"I see," his father said, his face falling. "I understand."

Justin took a deep breath. "Look, uh, Dad, maybe you could give me a hand with something."

"Sure. Sure, I could."

"Well, I bought a new spinnaker, and I haven't tried it out yet. I haven't taken her out since I brought her here, to tell you the truth. I thought maybe you and I could . . . you know, go for a sail." He ran his fingers through his hair, feeling awkward and stiff and strangely all right.

"Yeah," his father said in a voice almost too low to hear. "Maybe we could do that. You and I together."

Kate and Chelsea stood side by side at the end of the pier, looking out toward the dying sun. Chelsea held Connie in her arms. She was sleeping soundly, her little mouth working as she dreamed. Mooch stood by protectively.

"Some day," Chelsea said.

"Yes, it sure was," Kate agreed. "You okay?"

Chelsea considered for a moment. "I guess for someone who lost a husband and seems to have gained a child all in one morning, I'm fine."

"It was that kind of day all around," Kate remarked. She pointed toward the sailboat, its spinnaker unfurled, as it slipped before the sun, sails red. Two silhouettes were visible on the deck. "I think Justin gained a father."

Here's a sneak peek at
Making Waves #4: Thrill

"Oh, that's awful. It's an abomination. It's not possible that something so horrible could exist." Connor Riordan staggered back through the doorway, holding his hand over his face. "It's a crime against humanity, I tell you. And first thing in the morning!"

Chelsea Lennox glared at him impatiently. "Connor, it's only a dirty diaper. Get a grip." She handed him the used Pampers. "Then get rid of this."

"I can't, Chelsea," Connor pleaded. "I'll feed the little monster, I'll burp it. I'll even bathe it. But I can't—"

"Connor!" Chelsea snapped. "Take the diaper. Take it right now."

"Gak," the baby commented from her position on the coffee table.

Connor wrinkled his face miserably and lifted the corners of the diaper with two fingers. Then, holding his breath, he bolted from the room.

Once Connor was out of earshot, Chelsea allowed herself a groan. "If this is what it's like having kids, I think I'll pass. Permanently. Thank goodness the baby-sitter will be here in a few minutes. I actually look forward to going to work now."

Marta Salgado leaned forward in her wheelchair to pull a fresh diaper from the package. "Here," she said. "Don't forget the powder."

"I mean, it's night and day, night and day," Chelsea continued. "I haven't slept. I haven't gone out. Connor and I are spending half of what we earn on baby-sitters. And it's only been four days. Four days that seem like a lifetime."

"I don't see why Connie should be your problem," Marta said. "I mean, she's Connor's baby. Not yours."

"We don't even know that she's his," Chelsea said firmly. "That's what Molly said, but how much can you trust the word of a woman who'd run off and leave her own baby?"

Marta reached over to tickle the baby's foot. "Are you guys going to do a blood test?" she asked. "We can do it down at the clinic and find out pretty quickly if Connor's the father." She smiled. "Or not."

"Then what?" Chelsea finished diapering and lifted the baby into her arms. "I mean, if she isn't Connor's biological daughter, what do we do? Turn her over to an orphanage? She'll grow up being afraid to ask for more gruel. And when she finally gets out, she'll have to work as a pickpocket."

Marta laughed. "I think orphanages may have improved a bit since the days of Oliver Twist."

Chelsea looked down at the baby with a mixture of affection and annoyance. "You know, when Kate and I came to Ocean City for the summer, I was thinking fun, sun . . . guys with big shoulders. The last great fling before I sentence myself to four years of college, followed by a lifetime of work. I was *not* thinking, Hey, how about if I get engaged to an Irish illegal alien, come within about eight seconds of getting married, and then acquire a baby who may or may not be his?"

"Ahhh bvabva bva bva phh," the baby remarked.

"See, Connie's not thrilled about this, either," Chelsea said. "She's wondering why one minute her mother has pale skin and freckles and the next minute she's black. This can be very confusing."

"Maybe you should call the cops and have them track Molly down," Marta suggested. She held out her arms. "Here, I'll take her for a minute. You should try to grab some breakfast. But if she dumps again, she's all yours."

Connor came back into the living room, carrying a mug of tea. "We can't call the cops," he said. "For a start, I'm in the country illegally. And then there's the question of where they'd put the baby."

"Chelsea seems to think they'll put her in Dickensian England," Marta joked.

Connor flopped into the aging La-Z-Boy and tilted it back to half recline. He bent over to tie the laces of his work boots. "There's also the question of what they might do to Molly. I mean, she's a crazy, vengeful, stupid girl, but she's not actually evil. I don't believe she means to abandon it altogether."

"*It?*" Marta echoed.

"He's acting tough," Chelsea said in a loud stage whisper. "When they're alone, he talks goo-goo like everyone else."

"I do not!" Connor cried.

Alec Daniels wandered in from the kitchen. He was wearing a ratty Ocean City Beach Patrol T-shirt and red lifeguard trunks. "I believe the phrase I overheard last night was something along the lines of, 'Is Connie-wonnie gonna winky her bottle-wottle?'" He leaned over and gave Marta a kiss on her neck. "Of course," he added, grinning at Connor, "I also overheard the phrase, 'Don't you crap again, you little monster. Not if you want to see your first birthday.'"

"Speaking of which," Marta said, wrinkling her nose. She held the baby out toward Chelsea.

"I think it's Connor's turn," Chelsea said.

"Twice in ten minutes?" Connor demanded of Connie. "Twice in ten minutes? You're a bloody spawn of the devil."

"And who would know that better than you?" Chelsea said sweetly.

"Well, Marta and I are going running on the boardwalk," Alec said quickly.

"Running, in his case," Marta amended. "Rolling, in mine. Sorry, Connor. You're on your own."

"I'm in hell," Connor said glumly.

"Gak," Connie agreed.

Justin woke when Kate climbed out of bed to get ready for work. He hadn't heard the alarm, but the movement of sheets and the faint creak of springs had brought him to alertness. He lay still and quiet, enjoying the sight of Kate's body, lit by stray dusty beams of sunlight filtering through the one tiny window in the boathouse. She slipped on her terry-cloth robe and used both hands to tousle her sun-streaked blond hair. Every morning she went through the same routine before she went up to the main house to shower and dress.

"Hi," he said.

"Go back to sleep," Kate said. "You have the day off."

"Unfortunately, that doesn't mean I can sleep in," Justin said, yawning. He hooked his thumb toward his sailboat, rocking gently in the water below the loft. "Job number two." He grinned at her speculatively. "Of course, if you'd like to call in sick and stay here . . ."

Kate shook her head. "I don't think so. Shelby would kill me. We still have all kinds of prep work for the tournament."

"We both work too much," Justin said. "We should play more."

"Well, at least tomorrow you get to work with me on the catch-and-release tournament," Kate said. "That's pretty close to play."

The shark tournament was a big event for the Safe Seas Foundation, where Kate interned. It was an opportunity for the biologists to get a count on the dwindling shark population in the area. Workers from the foundation and volunteers from the Beach Patrol rode along with fishermen, tagging and weighing all sharks caught and then releasing them back into the Atlantic.

"I'll show you catch and release," Justin said, pulling her close. Kate put up a half-hearted struggle, then relaxed into his arms as he kissed her.

He tried to make it last, but she pulled away with a regretful smile. "I gotta go," she said. "Really."

"Don't let Shelby talk you into working late," Justin warned.

"Promise."

He watched her descend the stairway. "Hey," he called, pointing to some papers on the battered table that served as nightstand, dining-room table, and makeshift chair. "You need this stuff you were reading last night?"

Kate stopped on the stairs and glanced over her shoulder. "That? No. That's just some propaganda from Columbia."

Justin rolled out of bed and stretched. Below him, the boathouse door closed behind Kate. He reached for the papers on the table and scanned the top sheet. Columbia University Freshman Orientation Information, read the heading. Justin grimaced and tossed the papers aside. It was too early to ruin his day thinking about all that.

He walked across the narrow loft to the railing that overlooked his boat. The sailboat, its mast lying flat, nestled snugly between the wood catwalks, wallowing slightly from the wake of a passing speedboat.

Justin considered going back to bed and enjoying another hour's sleep, but the boat beckoned. A full day to get some work done. He didn't want to waste any of it.

He steeled himself for a cold, cramped shower on the boat. He'd given up using the shower at the house, now that it was even more of a zoo in the morning. Up until recently Grace, who had shared the downstairs bathroom with him, had never been awake before 10 A.M. But now that she worked a day job, he had to compete for access. And competing for bathroom time with a woman, he'd decided, was always a losing proposition.

A shower in his boat involved hunching over a steel sink in a room the size of a broom closet, head lowered, knees bent, elbows tight against his sides as he worked to aim the hand-held spray nozzle on all parts of his body. The pressure was weak, and the water was cool. Worst of all, he had stupidly mirrored one wall, which meant he had to watch himself while he shuffled and twisted and squirmed.

"Are you *sure* you want to sail around the world?" he muttered as he pried himself out of the shower and slipped on a pair of trunks.

Breakfast was a stale cinnamon bun that he popped in the microwave to soften. He swallowed the last of the roll, then picked up a complicated bit of machinery about the size of his two fists and ventured out into the bright day. Kate's convertible was already gone. He spotted Connor up ahead, carrying his hard hat and all but running from the house. Connor, Justin had observed, had developed a deep love of labor—right about the time he'd been stuck with the baby.

Justin headed south down the main drag. The sun was warm on his back, and the breeze was cool. Perfect day-off weather.

Still, there was something about the August sunlight that made him recall that wistful, end-of-summer feeling he used to get as a kid.

Todd's Discount Marine was five blocks away. It was a ramshackle two-story building on the bay, a bait shop in an earlier life. Todd, a beefy, middle-aged man with skin like leather and shockingly white hair, gave him a wave.

"You done with that carburetor already?" he asked.

Justin set the carburetor on the varnished wood counter. "Good as new. My personal guarantee."

Todd nodded. "Well, let's see, that's forty bucks' labor, which I believe knocks down the balance on your account to about five hundred and thirty-two bucks."

Justin winced. "Ouch."

Todd rolled his eyes. "What is it you need today?"

"I need an anchor."

"What for? You never take that boat anywhere."

"Thought I might take her out for a little overnight trip," Justin said. "Run up the coast a ways." He enjoyed the look of surprise on his friend's face.

"Damn, you must have been putting in a lot of hours," Todd said. "And you with that pretty girlfriend. You sure you have your priorities straight?"

"It's not so hard if you just give up sleeping," Justin said.

"It's your life," Todd said. He looked suspiciously at Justin. "If everything shakes down all right, what then? I know you. You're going to be like a bull at the gate."

"The plan is to wait till hurricane season's over, then head south to the Caribbean in October."

"Uh-huh. You're just dumb enough to take off early," Todd said, leaning on the counter. "Don't feed me your bull. Once that boat's ready . . ."

Justin shifted uneasily under Todd's gaze. It was true. Justin was dying to go. It was something he'd worked toward for more than a year, spending every dime on it, every spare minute.

Of course, there was Kate. She was planning on heading off to college at the end of August. But he'd already begun to formulate a plan of his own. He'd get the boat ready, convince her to come along for just the rest of the summer, and then . . . well, seriously, after she'd seen firsthand how great it was going to be, would she really still want to go to college?

"You going to sell me an anchor or give me a hard time?" Justin asked.

"I can do both at once," Todd said with a laugh. Then he grew serious. "I might have a little suggestion for you, though. You know about the Faial Follies?"

"The what?"

"I take that as a no," Todd said. "It's a race—in the broadest sense of the word. It's mostly weekend sailors and guys with more boat than skill. They start off from Nantucket and make the crossing to Faial."

"Where or what is Faial?" Justin asked.

"It's an island in the Azores chain. About two thousand miles, more or less, due east. All these boats assemble there for a few days of drinking beer and swapping lies, then some head on across to Europe, up toward England or southeast to the Canaries. Usually about a hundred boats or so."

Justin felt his hands clench at his sides. "Cross the Atlantic?" he whispered.

"You and I have sailed together for what, since you were twelve or so?" Todd shrugged. "I wouldn't suggest it if I didn't think you were sailor enough to do it. It's like being on a conveyor belt—you ride the Gulf Stream the whole way. Course, you'll need at least one crew."

Justin swallowed. He wiped his palms against his trunks. *Cross the Atlantic!*

"Anyway," Todd said, "it beats doing something stupid like getting impatient and heading south into the middle of a hurricane. With this race you'd at least have some company out there. Some dumb-ass real-estate tycoon with a million bucks' worth of boat to haul your sorry butt out of the drink."

"It's something to think about," Justin said, staring into blank space. *Europe!* He could spend the winter sailing the Mediterranean. He and Kate. France, Italy, Greece. How could she say no to that? What better education was there?

"Of course, you'd have to have your boat squared away," Todd said. "They sail from Nantucket in twenty-eight days. And you need time to get up there."

"Twenty-eight days?" Justin echoed.

"Yep," Todd said. He grinned. "Of course, you'll be needing an anchor."

Making Waves Surf Camp Sweepstakes
Official Rules

1. **Entry:** NO PURCHASE NECESSARY. A PURCHASE DOES NOT IMPROVE YOUR CHANCES OF WINNING. VOID WHERE PROHIBITED BY LAW. Enter by filling out an official registration form (pursuant to Alloy's Privacy Statement and the Children's Online Privacy Protection Act (COPPA) located at the "Making Waves Surf Camp" page at http://alloy.com. , or if you want to enter by mail, see below. If you are not an existing Alloy member, you will be asked to register for a free Alloy ID through on-screen directions which shall request your first and last name, mailing address, and email address. Sweepstakes begins June 15, 2001, at 12:01 AM Eastern time and ends November 30, 2001, at 11:59 PM Eastern time. Automated or robotic entries submitted by individuals or organizations will be disqualified. To enter by mail, send a 3x5 card on which you have hand-printed your first and last name, address, telephone number and email address (if available) to: "Making Waves Surf Camp" Sweepstakes Mail-ins, 151 West 26th Street, 11th Floor, New York, New York 10001. All mail-in entries must be postmarked by November 30, 2001, and received no later than December 6, 2001

2. **Privacy:** By entering the Sweepstakes, you agree to Alloy's use of your personal information as described in Alloy Online's Privacy Statement at http://alloy.com/company/privacy/.

3. **Eligibility:** Only legal U.S. residents thirteen years or older are eligible to enter this Sweepstakes. Employees of Alloy Online, Inc. ("Alloy"), their respective parents, their affiliates, subsidiaries, suppliers, printers, distributors, advertising and promotional agencies, prize suppliers and the immediate family or household members of each are not eligible to participate or win.

4. **Winner Selection:** The winner will be selected in a random drawing from among all eligible entries on December 7, 2001, to be conducted by Alloy designated judges, whose decisions are final. Winners will be notified by e-mail, or mail as applicable, on or about December 10, 2001. Odds of winning depend on the number of eligible entries received. The Winner (or, if a minor, the parent or legal guardian) may be required to execute and return an Affidavit of Eligibility and Liability/Publicity Release within fourteen (14) days following attempted notification, or the winner may forfeit the prize and an alternate winner may be selected. Any winner notification returned as undeliverable will result in prize forfeiture and an alternate winner shall be selected. No prize substitutions or transfers are permitted.

5. **Prize:**

One (1) Grand Prize / A Trip for Two at Paskowitz Surf Camp in Southern California – Winner will receive a trip for the winner and one companion for five (5) days at the Paskowitz Surf Camp in San Diego, California during the Summer of 2002. Trip includes roundtrip coach airfare, accommodations and meals at the camp, ground transportation between the camp and the airport. Travel times shall be determined by Alloy. Winner is responsible for incidental expenses. Alloy reserves the right to substitute the prize for another prize of equal or greater value. APPROXIMATE RETAIL VALUE: $6,000.

6. **General Conditions:** This Sweepstakes is governed by the laws of the United States. All federal, state and local laws and regulations apply. All taxes, fees, and surcharges are the sole responsibility of the prize winner.

Except where legally prohibited, each winner (and parent/legal guardian if winner is a minor) grants (and agrees to confirm that grant in writing) permission for Alloy and those acting under the authority of each to use such winner's name and likeness for all advertising and/or publicity, without notice, review, approval, or additional compensation. Entrants further agree that Alloy, their respective parents, subsidiaries and affiliated companies, advertising and promotion agencies, suppliers, printers, distributors, and the respective officers, directors, employees, representatives and agents of each will have no liability whatsoever for, and shall be held harmless by entrants (and parent/legal guardian if entrant is a minor) against, any and all liability for any injuries, loss or damage of any kind to persons, including death, or property damage resulting in whole or in part, directly or indirectly, from acceptance, possession, misuse or use of any prize, participation in this promotion, or while traveling to, preparing for or participating in any prize-related activity. Alloy expressly disclaims any responsibility or liability for injury or loss to any person or property relating to the delivery and/or subsequent use of the prizes awarded. Alloy makes no representation or warranty of any kind concerning the appearance, safety or performance of any prize awarded. Restrictions, conditions, and limitations apply. Alloy will not replace any lost or stolen prize items.

7. **Conduct:** By entering this Sweepstakes, entrants agree to be bound by these Official Rules. The Official Rules will be posted at the Sweepstakes Site throughout the Sweepstakes. Entrants further agree to be bound by the decisions of the judges, whose decisions are final and binding in all respects.

8. **Limitations of Liability:** Alloy is not responsible for any incorrect or inaccurate information, or any technical or human error which may occur in the processing of submissions in the Sweepstakes or any damage to entrant or user equipment. If, for any reason, the Sweepstakes is not capable of running as planned or is affected by events which corrupt or affect the proper conduct of this Sweepstakes, then Alloy reserves the right to cancel, terminate, modify or suspend the Sweepstakes.

9. **Winner's List:** The name of the Winner will be posted at Alloy.com by December 10, 2001 and is available by mail after December 10, 2001, by sending a self-addressed, stamped, #10 envelope to: Alloy, 151 West 26th Street, 11th floor, NY, NY 10001, attn: "Making Waves Surf Camp" Sweepstakes Winner. Residents of Vermont and Washington may omit postage.

10. **Official Rules:** For a mailed copy of the official game rules, send a self-addressed, stamped envelope (residents of Vermont may omit return postage) before June 24, 2001 to: Alloy, 151 West 26th Street, 11th floor, NY, NY 10001, attn: "Making Waves Surf Camp" Sweepstakes Rules.

11. **Sponsor:** Alloy is the sole sponsor of this Sweepstakes and is responsible for the fulfillment of the Prize.